BOOK THIRTY-

BARNABAS, QUENTIN AND THE VAMPIRE BEAUTY

Promised an operation to keep her forever thin, beautiful model Adele Marriot falls into the clutches of the evil Dr. Stefan Spivak who turns her instead into a vampire. Managing to escape, Adele flees to Collinwood seeking help.

At Collinwood, Barnabas and Quentin Collins come to Adele's aid. They take her to Dr. Julia Hoffman who begins to work on a cure. At last Adele feels there is hope she will be saved from the terrible curse.

Then Dr. Spivak's evil associates appear at Collinwood. Suddenly Adele is in terror once again. Her life is in danger. And Barnabas and Quentin must fight against the evil doctor's powers—or be destroyed themselves.

Hermes Press

Published by Hermes Press, an imprint of
Herman and Geer Communications, Inc.

Daniel Herman, Publisher
Troy Musguire, Production Manager
Eileen Sabrina Herman, Managing Editor
Alissa Fisher, Graphic Design
Kandice Hartner, Senior Editor

2100 Wilmington Road
Neshannock, Pennsylvania 16105
(724) 652-0511
www.HermesPress.com; info@hermespress.com

Book design by Eileen Sabrina Herman
First printing, 2022

LCCN applied for: 10 9 8 7 6 5 4 3 2 1 0
ISBN 978-1-61345-264-6
ISBN Limited Edition: 978-1-61345-274-5
OCR and text editing by H + G Media and Eileen Sabrina Herman
Proof reading by Eileen Sabrina Herman and Feytaline McKinley

From Dan, Sabrina, and Jacob in memory of Al DeVivo

Acknowledgments: This book would not be possible without the help and encouragement of Jim Pierson and Curtis Holdings

Printed in Canada

Barnabas, Quentin and the Vampire Beauty
by Marilyn Ross

CONTENTS

CHAPTER 1

Midnight! The moment when night ends and the first dark hours of the morning begin – the dark hours that come with sinister quiet in which the unnamed monsters of the shadows venture forth and do their evil. It is an eerie time when much of the world's people are in that uncanny, comatose state known as sleep, and asleep become easy prey for the lost souls haunting the darkness with grim intent.

The werewolves and the vampires desert their coffins to stalk these sinister hours. All the creatures of the night descend to make their forays on the innocent! Occasional weird cries echo in the distant hills and valleys of the countryside. And in the great cities, sinister shadows emerge from the secrecy of dark retreats and prowl the deserted streets in search of victims.

Adele Marriot was dreaming of those midnight streets and a dark figure stalking her down a narrow, dead-end alley in Soho. Suddenly she was trapped and she turned to raise her hands protectively and cry out in fear as a phantom of the shadows bore down on her.

At that instant she awoke with a scream and sat up in bed. The room was small and bleak, with the bare furnishings one would expect in a modest private hospital. The pale moonbeams filtered in around the drawn blind and closed curtains of the room to give it a faint, cold light. It took her a moment to realize she'd been dreaming and know where she was. And the awakening brought no relief of her fear. She was beginning to be terrified of the Stemen Clinic and its suave, mysterious head, the gray-haired Dr. Stefan Spivak.

She heard a footstep outside her door and her heart began to pound. Then the door slowly opened and a gaunt-faced woman in a nurse's uniform stepped into the room. She was one of the several English nurses in this private hospital situated in a mountain village outside Zurich. Though all the Swiss nurses spoke English well enough, Adele felt more at ease with these countrywomen of hers. This particular nurse, Miss Chisholm, came from Adele's own London.

"Are you all right, Miss Marriot?" Nurse Chisholm asked in her slightly nasal tone with a hint of a Cockney accent in it.

"Yes," she replied in a small voice. "I had a bad dream. I woke up with a start."

The nurse was annoyed. "You must try to control your nerves, Miss Marriot. Dr. Spivak doesn't like any upset. There are other patients in the rooms all along this corridor."

"I know," she said in a near whisper.

The nurse hesitated a moment longer. "You're feeling better now?"

"Yes, thank you," she said hesitantly. "When will Dr. Spivak return from Paris?"

"Tomorrow morning, I believe," Nurse Chisholm said.

"I must talk to him then," Adele said nervously. "I'm very worried."

The nurse's gaunt face showed no sympathy. "I'm sure you have no reason to be. If you find it difficult to sleep, ring the bell and I'll come back with a sedative."

"Thank you," Adele said. "I think I'll be all right."

Nurse Chisholm went out again and closed the door after her. Adele lay back in her bed and stared up at the ceiling. She was trembling as if she'd experienced a chill. And in a way she had, a chill of fear. She had been on the verge of telling the nurse that the reason for her abject state was that she had gradually become afraid of the clinic. She was especially afraid of the tall, debonair doctor who was its head.

Staring up at the shadows, she went back to the first time she'd met Dr. Stefan Spivak. After wearying months in London as a photographer's model, she had come to Switzerland for a skiing holiday. She knew her oval-faced, calm beauty depended on rested nerves, so she felt the holiday to be a must. She bought a suitable wardrobe to set off her willowy figure, blonde hair and large green eyes. And then it was a plane to Zurich and a rented car to an Alpine village not too distant from the great city. There amid the snow-capped mountains she found peace and exciting outdoor recreation. The Pension Leonhard supplied good rooms and beds in a log-cabin sort of atmosphere and the meals were excellent. It was more a rural retreat than a smart hotel resort, but it was a pleasant change for her after London.

In the evenings there was dancing to accordion music in the big main room with its blazing fireplace. Tables were set out and people enjoyed refreshments and either danced or watched the dancers. Often Adele would be invited to dance, but a good deal of the time she sat alone at a small table and smilingly watched the festivities.

It was on her fourth evening at the Pension Leonhard that she first spotted the tall, elegant Dr. Stefan Spivak. He was the type who would stand out anywhere, and his perfectly-cut tweed suit singled him from the other men in ordinary sports clothes, some even in their rough open-collared shirts.

He was standing with the proprietor of the pension and they were both staring at her with obvious interest and saying something about her. Embarrassed, she pretended not to see them and gave her full attention to watching the dancers.

After a moment the stout proprietor came to her apologetically and said, "Miss Marriot, pardon my intrusion, but I have a distinguished guest who would much like to meet you."

"Oh?" she hesitated.

The stout man wiped his hands on his white apron in a manner which revealed his tension. "He is a man respected in medical circles all over the world and he has his clinic here. His name is Dr. Stefan Spivak."

She smiled. "Why should he want to meet me?"

"He considers you a great beauty. And the doctor is an admirer of female beauty."

It was a flattering compliment and she turned to glance at the tall doctor staring at her from the position he'd taken near the doorway. Paying no attention to the noise of the music and general hilarity, he returned her smile. And then he came across the room toward her, dodging the frantic dancers.

The innkeeper beamed as the suave Dr. Spivak bowed to her and then introduced him, saying, "This is the noted Dr. Stefan Spivak of the famed Stemen Clinic near here. May I present Miss Adele Marriot."

"Charmed to meet you, Miss Marriot," the swarthy, lean doctor said, taking her hand in his and kissing it. "May I sit down?"

"Please do," she said as the innkeeper discreetly withdrew. The doctor said, "I hope you don't resent my interest in you."

Her eyes twinkled. "I'm somewhat baffled by it."

"But you oughtn't to be," Dr. Spivak said, leaning close to her at the table so he could be heard easily. "You are the most beautiful young woman to show up in this place."

"I'm sure you're exaggerating," Adele protested.

"Not a whit," the doctor told her in his precise, slightly accented English. "And you are a Britisher. You are no doubt in the theater or perhaps in films?"

"Neither," she told him with a smile. "I'm a model. A photographer's model. I pose mostly for fashion advertisements. I thought you might have seen me in one of them. Often they appear in European magazines."

His eyes brightened. "Of course. That is why you seemed so familiar to me. What an excellent surprise. So you have come here for a holiday and some skiing?"

"Yes," she said. "I'm between jobs. And I needed a rest and change. I had been on a strenuous diet and it has left me feeling weak and ill."

The tall doctor was listening closely. She judged him to be in his late forties. His dark, shiny hair was receding at the temples and he had a lean, hawk-like face. His black, gleaming eyes were particularly interesting with a hint of the hypnotic about them.

He said, "It's a coincidence that you should speak of dieting. It happens that my work is in that field."

Her eyebrows raised. "Really?"

"Yes. If I may say so, the Stemen Clinic is rather successful for its work in curing patients with weight problems."

"Please tell me about it. You don't know how I torment and starve myself to keep my figure."

"We have a different approach to overweight than dieting."

"What sort of approach?"

"Surgical. I do an operation on the pituitary gland which cures any tendencies to obesity. This gland controls so many of the important body functions, and I have discovered a technique by which it can also permanently regulate the body so that a patient remains slim."

"That's fantastic!"

The doctor smiled modestly. "It is a minor contribution to medicine and I find it necessary to keep the operative procedure an expensive one. But it has helped many prominent people who have been able to afford it, and I'm sure it would benefit you."

The music continued in the background as she said, "I only

wish I could have the operation. How long does it take?"

"A month from the day you'd enter my clinic until the day you leave it."

She showed surprise. "That isn't long. I could afford the time. But I couldn't afford your fee, I'm sure of that. I'm only a poor working girl." She laughed ruefully.

There was a strange, speculative look in his hypnotic black eyes as he studied her. "Suppose I offered you the operation without a fee?"

"You're joking!"

"No," he said. "I will treat you free of charge if you wish to place yourself in my hands. And all that I ask in payment is that you tell your friends about my clinic when you return to London. It is not considered ethical for me to advertise, so I depend on word of mouth to spread the news about my work and bring me customers. You must know many well-to-do people in the arts, stage and film circles in London who would be happy to learn of my services."

Adele nodded. "I do know a lot of people, many who could afford your clinic. And I'd be glad to tell them about you."

Dr. Stefan Spivak smiled. "Think it over then. I have an opening at the clinic now. I'll hold the room for a few days while you consider. And if you decide to take advantage of my offer, it will cost you nothing."

She said, "Is it a dangerous operation?"

"No. Difficult, yes. With the pituitary there is always a risk. But if the gland is normal, you should come out of it with flying colors. Do you have any close family back home in England? I mean anyone you should consult?"

She shook her head. "Both my parents are dead. I was an only child. I have a distant cousin, but I only hear from her at Christmas."

The doctor smiled sympathetically. "No family. Well, that is both bad and good. Surely, a young woman as beautiful as you must have a boyfriend?"

She blushed. "I'm engaged. To a newspaper photographer. He was planning to come here on this holiday with me, but something came up to keep him in London. His name is Douglas Edwards. He published a book of photos on the Thames a year ago."

"Interesting. Of course you'd have to discuss the operation with him."

"Yes," she agreed. "But I could phone him if I decide."

Dr. Spivak smiled again. "Don't make any rash decisions about this. But I feel I had to make my offer. I think it might spare you many problems in the future."

"I'll certainly think about it," she promised.

"Good," he said. "And in the meantime, perhaps you'll extend the pleasure of your company to me when I have a few hours to spare. I'd enjoy dancing with you now."

A moment later she was in his arms whirling about the wooden floor to the tuneful accordion music. The flames in the fireplace leaped before her excited eyes as he whirled her past them, and she felt he was perhaps the most fascinating man she'd ever met.

This conviction endured in the days and nights that followed. For the medical chief of an important private clinic, he managed to get a good many hours free. He met her for skiing during the day and for dinner and dancing at night. Once they visited in nearby Zurich, where they attended a nightclub, and one sunny afternoon he drove her up in the mountains and showed her his hospital.

Located on a scenic spot high in the white-clad mountains, it was built like a great stone castle and somewhat smaller than she'd expected. Smoke curled upward from its chimneys but there were no signs of movement or life about the place. It appeared deserted.

She turned in the small sports car and asked him, "Why are there no people about?"

"I require that my patients rest a great deal," he said. "And I do not encourage visitors. At least not until my patients are ready to leave. Only the few tradespeople who have deliveries to make disturb the quiet. It is a place for treatment and rest."

This seemed a valid enough explanation, although there had been a ghostly atmosphere about the isolated castle which had worried her. It seemed so far away from the nearest village and so strangely quiet. But to balance her uneasiness there was the warm charm of Dr. Stefan Spivak. She had come to have great friendliness for him and confidence in his ability.

It was his personality which made her decide to risk the operation. So she phoned London the day before she was to leave the pension and enter the clinic. After much difficulty she managed to get through to Douglas at his newspaper office. Quickly she explained what she was proposing to do.

"Wait a minute," he begged her. "Don't get too excited about this. Shouldn't you first try to find out about this doctor and who he has operated on?"

"He's treated dozens of famous people," she assured him. "And a lot of ones not so well known. But they don't allow him to use their names for advertising. They don't want people to know they've had weight problems. It's embarrassing."

"It would be more than embarrassing if the operation isn't a success," the worried young man warned.

"In any case it can't hurt me," she told him. "The worst that could happen would be that it won't help."

"But the pituitary gland," he said, "is a very tricky area to meddle with. Are you sure he knows what he is doing?"

"He's famous," she chided Douglas. "And extremely nice. And he has a very large clinic. I'm lucky to have the chance of a free operation."

"I'd like to see you and discuss it first!"

"No time for that," she said. "I have to enter the clinic tomorrow. But you can come for me when I leave. We'll have a few days here and then go back to London. You can meet me here in a month. I'll let you know."

The young man at the other end of the line sounded concerned. "I think you're rushing into this too fast. Can't you take a little more time to consider it?"

"No. Dr. Spivak has only one room vacant at the hospital now," she said. "If I don't accept his offer I'll lose the opportunity."

"Better to risk that," Douglas insisted.

"No. I've made up my mind," she said firmly. "Please don't try to make me change it. I'll either write or phone when I want you to come and meet me for the journey back to London."

The young man's final comment was, "I don't like it at all!"

Adele was a little upset by his reaction to her decision. But she had no intention of allowing it to stop her. She settled her bill at the pension the following afternoon and Dr. Spivak made a special trip in his sleek little sports car to pick her up and take her to the hospital.

On the drive there she found him in a more serious mood than before, and she put this down to the fact that they were now changing their relationship to that of doctor and patient. She felt she understood why he was suddenly more restrained.

As they reached the more isolated snow-lined road which led to the castle-like building, he spoke to her. "You may find the hospital rather different at first."

"Oh?" She glanced at his hawk-like profile.

The swarthy man kept his eyes on the road. "During the daytime we do not encourage patients to leave their rooms and mingle. Though on certain nights we do have formal parties for newcomers. But these are rare."

"I see," she said.

"My policy is for the patients' benefit," he assured her.

"Of course," she said.

"You may also find the hospital austere and plain by your standards," he said. "But remember, many wealthy and prominent people come to me not for the luxury of the surroundings but for the cure that I can offer."

"I understand," she told him.

For she was not in the mood to question him about anything. She had put her faith in his ability and now she would do what he said without hesitation. There was no other way. All doctors asked the same confidence in their decisions and none of them offered any more promise of a successful treatment than did Dr. Stefan Spivak.

As they neared the hospital a wind and snowstorm came up. The sky had darkened gradually until it was almost pitch dark, and the blinding snow came hurtling before the beam of the headlights, making it nearly impossible to see. At the same time the wind whistled weirdly around the little car and actually swerved it occasionally.

The doctor had long ago put on the headlights and now she turned to study him in the faint light from the dashboard and ask, "Are sudden storms like this a regular thing?"

His eyes were straining to see ahead. "They can happen. It's what mountain climbers have to beware of. If they get caught near the peak they can be trapped there and die of exposure if there are no huts close by."

She shivered a little at the ominous weather outside the little car and worried that they might get bogged down in a drift. She said, "Is there any danger of missing the road or getting stuck in the deep snow?"

"No," he said curtly. "We'll be there in a few minutes." And then, just after that, she saw the blurred lantern light marking the entrance of the castle ahead. He halted the car by the door and helped her through the blowing snow to the front steps. At once the huge door swung open and Adele saw Nurse Chisholm's gaunt face for the first time. The English nurse was holding a candle.

"Good evening, Doctor," she said. "The lights have cut out again. The storm, I suppose."

"Yes," he frowned. "This is a new patient, Miss Adele Marriot. This is Nurse Chisholm."

They acknowledged his introduction and then Nurse Chisholm led them down a long, deserted stone corridor.

There were wooden doors with rounded tops opening off the corridor at regular intervals. Almost at the end of the hall the nurse halted before one of these doors and opened it.

At Adele's side, Dr. Spivak said, "This will be your room while you're here."

"Thank you," she said, and rather timidly entered it. Her first reaction was that it was small and cold. Nurse Chisholm used her candle to light one set in a holder on the dresser. Adele surveyed the iron-frame bed, the cheap dresser and the two plain chairs which comprised the furniture of the room. The doctor had not been wrong in warning her that it would be plain. It was very plain indeed!

Dr. Spivak had moved over to a wooden clothes closet which was installed in a corner of the stone-walled room. He gave her a cold smile. "Not large enough for your wardrobe, I'm afraid. But you'll need only a dress or two here and you need not unpack everything."

"No," she said, feeling let down and a little frightened. Had she been too quick to make her decision to come to this place?

Dr. Spivak said, "Your dinner will be served here. Plain food but good enough. I'd like to eat with you but I have many things to look after and we have no communal dining room here. All food is served in the patient's room."

"Thank you," she said with a wan smile. "I hope I'll soon learn the rules."

"Miss Chisholm will be a great help to you in that regard," Dr. Spivak said. "I'll be visiting you here in the morning to take certain tests. Good night. I hope you sleep well."

"I'm tired enough," she said.

He nodded, and some of the charm she'd come to expect showed once again. He said, "You'll find this all new and alarming. That's, true of any hospital or clinic. Just be patient until you adjust."

"I will," she promised.

He smiled. "Until the morning then."

And she was left alone in the cold candlelit room. Outside the small window of leaded glass the wind howled in terrifying fashion and the snow pelted against the panes.

She drew her coat about her and glanced at the bed to see if there were enough blankets. There didn't seem too many. A mood of melancholy and uneasiness took hold of her.

She went to the dresser and studied herself in the mirror by the candlelight. She thought that she looked very pale and weary. The strain of the long drive and worry about her decision to come to the clinic clearly showed on her pretty face.

The door opened again and it was Nurse Chisholm with her bags. The thin nurse set them down and gave her a curious appraisal. "You're from London," she said.

"Yes."

"I was born there," the nurse said.

"So was I," Adele told her.

The bony face was grim. "I'll be back shortly with your food tray."

"Do we have any choice?"

"Not here," Nurse Chisholm told her. "The doctor is very strict about what the patients eat."

When the nurse left her again, she started to unpack. It took her a little while, as she had to select which things to take from the suitcases and which to leave in them. She was just finishing when Nurse Chisholm returned with a tray containing a glass of milk, cheese and black bread.

"Don't complain," Nurse Chisholm warned her. "It's what everyone gets."

She glanced at the Spartan fare in dismay. "Nothing warm?"

The nurse shook her head. "That's it. If you want anything else you can ask the doctor when you see him in the morning."

"I'm so chilled," Adele said. "A warm drink would help me."

"Talk to the doctor tomorrow," Nurse Chisholm said in her brusque fashion and she left the room again.

Keeping her coat around her shoulders, Adele sat down with the tray on her bed. She was hungry as well as chilled, and the food tasted good. The drab little room and thin fare were a contrast to the warmth of her quarters at the pension and the excellent food she'd enjoyed there. But this was a hospital and she was being given an expensive operation free of charge. An operation which would allow her to keep her glamorous figure without having to starve herself relentlessly as in the past. Too bad that she couldn't at least gorge herself now that the operation would take care of any problems of weight. But there would be lots of opportunity for gourmet meals later.

She finished everything on the tray and then placed it on the dresser. The wind continued to howl outside and hail beat against the window. A draft crossed the room and caused the single candle to flicker so wildly that she feared it might go out. She turned to discover the sudden cool breeze was caused by the opening of the hallway door. A girl was standing in the doorway.

"Hello," she said in a throaty voice. "You're new here, aren't you?"

Adele stared at her. "Yes, I am."

The girl came into the room. She was a beauty with dark, upswept hair and she wore a low-cut dress of black velvet with white lace trim. The strange thing was that the dress seemed of another period. It was the sort Adele had seen in paintings a hundred to a hundred and fifty years old. Another strange thing was the contrast between the girl's chalk white face and the redness of her lips. The lips were thick in contrast to the girl's delicate face and had a wet, bloody look. She had a dark mole in the middle of her left cheek and heavy black arched eyebrows. Her eyes were also unusual, with their burning, feverish glitter.

The girl eyed her up and down. "You're here for the operation?"

"Yes. Are you?"

The lovely dark girl chuckled. "What else? I'm weary of wandering as I am. Have they found you an opposite yet?"

Adele frowned. "An opposite?"

"Of course. You must have an opposite or it's no good."

"I don't understand," she confessed.

The dark girl in the velvet dress stared at her in surprise. "Then if you don't know about it you must be an opposite! That's amusing! Truly amusing." And she laughed.

"Please explain," Adele said.

The girl waved a hand impatiently. "It isn't all that important, my dear. You'll find out soon enough." And she crossed the room to examine Adele's dresses. As she riffled through them on the hangers, she exclaimed, "What strange styles!"

Adele was about to protest that they were the latest in fashion when a frightening thing happened. She looked into the dresser mirror which reflected the area of the clothes closet. She saw the closet but there was no image of the girl in the mirror. She was startled and put it down to an optical illusion. But before she could wonder any further the door to her room was thrown open and an angry Dr. Stefan Spivak burst in. He saw the girl and went straight across to her and grasped her roughly by the arm.

She turned and looked terrified. "I didn't do anything."

Dr. Spivak told the dark girl, "I have warned you before about wandering."

The girl struggled to free herself from his grip. "Ask her. She'll tell you! I just came in here a moment ago! I didn't bother her!"

"We'll discuss that later," he said angrily. "Just now I'm taking you back to your own room." And with that he dragged the protesting girl out. He closed the door after them and left Adele standing alone in the tiny room again.

The whole episode had been baffling. And the doctor had been so enraged he hadn't even spoken to her. But why be so upset because the dark girl had left her room? What harm could there be in that? It seemed ridiculous that he should make such a fuss about it.

She was debating all this in her mind when from a distant area of the house there came a wild, piercing scream, followed by the silence which seemed to perpetually mantle the gray old castle.

CHAPTER 2

Nurse Chisholm came early with her breakfast tray. Adele had slept badly during the night. The frightening scream she'd heard just before going to bed had upset her nerves and the cold of the tiny bedroom hadn't helped. At least there was warm porridge, steaming hot tea and the familiar black bread on the tray.

She told the nurse, "I'm cold. I have been all night."

The grim-faced Nurse Chisholm turned from the breakfast tray which she'd left on the dresser and asked, "Why did you come here?"

Adele was surprised. "For the operation, of course."

"You really want it?"

"Yes," she said. "I'm tired of never being able to eat as much as I want and of having to exercise continually to keep my weight down."

The nurse smiled mockingly. "And you think Dr. Spivak offers you an easy way to avoid extra pounds?"

"His operation is a success."

"Did he explain it all to you?" the nurse wanted to know.

"Of course."

"I wouldn't look for miracles if I were you," the nurse said. "But don't tell him I said so. If I were you, I'd pack my bags and leave at once."

Adele frowned. "You can't mean that? He's given me a wonderful opportunity. I'm to have the operation for nothing."

Nurse Chisholm showed no expression. "I've said what I think. Don't ever say I didn't warn you. But you're like the rest of them. Too vain to care about anything but your beauty." And with that pronouncement she went on her way.

Adele wasn't taken with the grim-faced nurse. It would be too much to expect her to understand the things you went through for beauty. The operation might be difficult but it would be over within a short while. The alternative was for her to go on fasting for years. She'd had enough of that. Even if the operation was unpleasant she'd prefer it, especially since Dr. Spivak had assured her there would be no risks.

After breakfast she paced restlessly in the cell-like room waiting for the doctor to call on her. Sun was shining in through the single small window; though it brought little warmth, at least it made her feel better. There was a light knock on her door and she opened it to see Dr. Spivak standing there.

The tall, swarthy man was wearing a doctor's white smock and there was a stethoscope around his neck. He seemed in a much different humor than he had been on the previous night when he'd literally dragged the dark girl from her room.

Entering the room he said, "I see you have your coat on your shoulders. Are you cold?"

"Yes. I have been all night."

"I'm sorry," he said. "We were at a disadvantage with the electricity off." He went to the wall and switched on a plain white globe mounted close to the high ceiling to provide light in the room. "It is on now. And I'll have Nurse Chisholm bring you a portable electric heater. It will make it much more comfortable in here."

"Thank you," she said. "I realize you had problems last night with the electricity gone and the storm."

"That is true."

"You needn't have worried about that girl coming into my room," Adele went on. "She didn't bother me."

His hawk-like face hardened. "She broke a rule. I don't encourage that."

"I hope you weren't too stern with her on my account."

"I promise you I wasn't," he said.

"I hadn't much chance to talk with her," she went on. "But I rather enjoyed her company."

"Lisa can be entertaining when she likes," Dr. Stefan Spivak said stiffly. "But she is being readied for an operation and she shouldn't have been out of her own room."

"She's a strange girl. Dresses like someone from another age."

His hypnotic eyes were fixed on her. "You noticed that?"

"I couldn't help it. Why does she dress that way?"

"She is rather eccentric, very wealthy and able to indulge her whims. Most of my patients have those things in common, they are wealthy and peculiar. So you can understand what a pleasant change you are for me."

She smiled. "Is that why you are doing my operation without charge?"

He nodded. "Because I like you a great deal."

"And I'm grateful," she said. "Lisa spoke to me about opposites. I think she asked me if I had an opposite. What did she mean?"

His thin face shadowed. "She often talks nonsense."

"But she must have meant something," Adele insisted.

He shrugged. "I'll have to ask her. I can supply no answer at the moment. She often speaks in riddles."

"How long before you operate on me?" she asked.

He took a few carefully wrapped items from the pocket of his smock. "I can tell you better after I've taken a sample of your blood. I'm going to do that now. If your blood stands up to the test well, I would expect you to be on the operating table within a few days."

"I'm anxious to get it over with."

"I understand," he said, preparing a needle to withdraw blood from her arm. "Now if you will just be still for a moment."

He took the sample of blood and then wrapped the items again. He seemed about ready to leave, but she wanted to talk to him a little longer and find out more about the clinic.

She said, "It seems quieter here in the daytime than it is at night. I should think there would be more activity."

His weird, burning eyes met hers. "On the contrary, it is part of my method of treatment to have my patients sleep during the daylight hours. The hospital is much more alive at night."

"And you still don't encourage the patients to socialize then?"

"Only on rare occasions," the doctor said. "Our business here is to bring about a change in physical condition. Every effort is directed toward that."

"I can't get used to the silence and being alone," she said. "I feel as if I were in prison. Can't I go out for a walk in the snow?"

"You can if you go alone and restrict yourself to the clinic grounds," he said.

"I'm perfectly willing to do that," she said.

"Fine. I'll tell Nurse Chisholm to take you to the side door when you're ready," Dr. Spivak said. "But don't stay out too long. It's cold and blustery after the big storm."

"I promise to be back within an hour," she said.

"Less would be better. You'll find it cold out there. Even in your skiing clothes."

She smiled. "I don't suppose you have time to take me to the nearest ski slope today?"

He looked resigned. "I'm sorry to have to say no. But another time perhaps."

"I hope so," she said.

He started to the door and turned to say, "I'll have Nurse Chisholm bring you the heater at once."

With that assurance he left her. She hoped to ask him about the scream but decided she would let it go until they met again. She hadn't wanted to get him in a mood by asking too many questions. He might even venture an explanation of his own free will later on. This thought she allowed to comfort her.

She had changed into a red ski outfit with white trim and was ready to leave by the time Nurse Chisholm arrived with an ancient electric heater which had a coil in the middle of a reflector. The nurse moodily plugged it into a wall socket near her.

"The doctor said to leave it on all the time," the nurse told her as she picked up the empty breakfast tray. "That should warm it."

"I'm positive it will," she said. "Now will you show me the nearest exit?"

Nurse Chisholm eyed her suspiciously. "Did Dr. Spivak say you could go out?"

"Yes. He promised that you'd direct me to the nearest door."

"Very well, come with me," the older woman said. And she led her out into the high-ceilinged corridor, shadowed and gloomy even in the daylight.

"This must be a very old building," Adele said as she walked along the stone floor beside the nurse.

"Goes back three hundred years," Nurse Chisholm said. "The doctor got it very cheap from the last of the family who owned it. Most of the others had died earlier, a lot of them suicides. And there's a nasty legend in this district that the castle is haunted."

"A haunted hospital," Adele said lightly. "That is something different."

Nurse Chisholm gave her a strange look. "You don't know anything about this place yet."

"But I shall before I leave," she pointed out.

"No doubt," the nurse said grimly. She indicated the end of the hallway. "There's a door to the courtyard out there. Don't wander away too far and use the same door when you return. Do you think you can find your way to your room alone?"

She nodded. "Yes. I took careful note of the way we came."

"When you come in go straight to your room," the nurse

said. "The doctor won't want you wandering through the building."

"I know that," she said. "Lisa visited my room last night and he was very angry with her."

"Lisa?"

"Yes. You know her? She's a patient waiting for an operation."

"I know her," Nurse Chisholm said in her dour fashion. "You watch out for her. And I don't blame the doctor for being angry." She turned and vanished down another corridor on the left.

Adele went out into the wintery morning. She was surprised that they all had such a poor opinion of Lisa. Though eccentric, Lisa seemed a nice enough girl. She opened the heavy oaken door and ventured out onto the stone steps. From where she stood, the old castle looked more like a storybook structure than a modern hospital.

Its windows were tiny, some of them barred. It had great turrets on its roof and there was a courtyard with an arched stone exit leading to the grounds outside. She went down the steps, her breath showing like vapor in the cold air, and walked across the courtyard toward the gate.

She stood outside the gate surveying the majestic mountains which rose up on all sides around the ancient castle. It was a breathtaking scene, and she enjoyed the view and the fresh air.

Then she heard crunching footsteps in the snow to her left and turned to see a young man in warm winter garb with a fur hat that came down over his ears. He was carrying some parcels.

She said, "Do you work for Dr. Spivak?"

The boy nodded and in a thickly accented voice said, "I work for clinic."

"Are you from the village?" she wanted to know.

"I live in village when I am not working here," he said.

"Are there many employed in the clinic?"

The youth looked uneasy. "I don't know," he said. "I bring parcels up from the train. I shovel the snow in winter and do the gardens in summer."

She smiled at him. "You are kept busy."

"I am," he said. And he moved on.

As he went through the arch into the courtyard she watched after him. She had the impression that he was either afraid to talk to her or was mentally dull. She couldn't be sure which. Yet he seemed to speak English very well. It seemed that everything and everyone about the hospital were vague and mysterious. Perhaps this was the result of the clinic's patients wanting their operations to be kept so secret.

She walked a distance down the path in the snow the youth

had used. And at last she could see the village far below in a valley. There were the usual cluster of houses and the spire of a church. She was so high, the tracks of a railway running through the village looked as if they were part of a toy train set. It made her feel better to know that the clinic wasn't completely isolated, that close by there was a village.

After standing there a few moments she decided to start back. The prospect of the heater in her room was inviting. And since it was the rule of the hospital for the patients to sleep in the daylight hours, she thought she might take a nap to make up for her lost sleep the night before. She still worried about that scream and whether it had come from the unfortunate Lisa.

She walked across the courtyard and was about to enter the silent building when there was a sudden tapping on a window directly over the door. She looked up and was able to make out the smiling face of a rather pretty girl staring down at her. She felt it a happy omen that the girl was there and waved to her. The girl responded and made signs to indicate that they would meet on the inside. Adele nodded and then went up the stone steps and into the old building.

She walked along the corridor slowly, expecting the girl to join her at any moment. But there was no sign of her. Disappointed, she finally came to the door of her own room and went inside. At once she could feel the results from the ancient electric heater. She took off her coat and knitted cap and was about to hang them up when the door slowly opened and the girl she'd seen from the window came in. The girl put a finger to her lips to warn her against speaking out until she'd gently closed the door.

Then the girl rushed over to the old heater and held her hands in front of it to warm them. "Isn't that divine!" she exclaimed. She was rather stout, with a pretty face, but her hair was a mousy brown color. She wore a dark pants suit and looked and sounded like an American. She smiled at Adele, still bent before the heater. "My name is Helen," she said. "I'm a Yank stranded in Europe. My folks won't send me any money unless I promise to go home and give up the hippie bit. And I won't do it!"

"A capsule history of yourself." Adele smiled at the teenager. "I wish I could do as well."

"You're English, you don't have to tell me that," the girl said. "What are you doing here?"

"I'm a patient of the clinic," Adele said. "What about you?"

"So am I," Helen said. "I guess you can see I'm overweight. Dr. Spivak is giving me my operation free in return for my working as his secretary for a few months. I can type and it will give me a place to live so I bought the idea. I'm having my operation tonight."

"Tonight?" she exclaimed. "Does the doctor operate at night?"

"Always," the American girl said. "Everything important around here seems to happen at night. It's the only time you ever see anyone walking around. And the doctor is terribly strict. He likes everyone to stay in their rooms unless they have permission from him to leave them. He'd be in a rage if he found me here now."

"I know," Adele agreed. "A girl named Lisa came in here last night and he caught her. He was very angry."

"Lisa," the girl repeated the name. "I haven't met her but I think I've heard her name mentioned."

Adele stared at the other girl. "Are you afraid of the operation?"

"No," Helen said cheerfully. "The doctor has promised me it won't hurt and it will keep me nice and thin for the rest of my life. Maybe I can get myself a flock of new boy friends."

Adele smiled. "I hope so."

"Did you see the boy from the village who brings the parcels from the post office? Isn't he nice?"

"He seemed very nice. But not too talkative."

Elelen nodded knowingly. "You can bet the doctor has warned him about being friendly with us."

"Why?"

The teenager sighed. "I have an idea most of his patients are wealthy and famous. They don't want people to know they've come here for the operation. So it all has to be very hush-hush."

"It makes me a little nervous," Adele admitted.

"Don't worry about it," Helen said. "I think Dr. Spivak is wonderful. And that first name of his, Stefan! If he were younger I'd set my cap for him. You should try it."

Adele shook her head. "I'm already engaged to someone."

"No wonder," the stout girl said. "You're pretty."

Adele smiled. "Thank you. How long does it take after the operation before you're able to be up and around?"

"Dr. Spivak says most of the patients are able to get up and walk a little after three days or so. But he keeps them here for almost a month to be sure there has been a cure."

"Then you should be able to tell me all about it before my operation," Adele said.

"Likely. I'd better get back to my own room now before they catch me here."

"I suppose so," Adele agreed.

Helen left the heater and made a wry face. "That awful old Nurse Chisholm loves to tell tales. If she saw me here she'd go straight to the doctor."

"He has strict rules as you said," Adele reminded her.

The vivacious Helen smiled again. "Right. So I'll be on my way. And as soon as I'm over the operation I'll come by and tell you just what it was like."

"I'll count on that," she said.

It was the last real talk she was ever to have with the jolly American girl. The next time she saw Helen was to be under totally different circumstances. But she knew nothing of those things then.

She was fairly comfortable in her room, and when she asked Nurse Chisholm for newspapers and magazines she was brought a sampling of the best English periodicals. This helped her wile away the long hours. And she became more adjusted to the odd quiet of the old castle.

The second day of her stay at Stemen Clinic she was again visited by Dr. Stefan Spivak. He seemed in a good humor as he told her, "Your blood tests were most satisfactory. I plan to operate on you within the week."

"I'm writing to my fiance," she said. "Nurse Chisholm promised she would mail the letter for me."

"Of course," the doctor said.

"When will I tell him to come here to meet me and take me back to London?" she asked.

Dr. Spivak rubbed his chin. "Tell him the end of the month. That's about twenty-four days from now."

"It will.take that long?"

"I'll really be rushing you out of here then," the hawk-faced doctor said. "But as long as you'll have someone to accompany you, I'll take the chance. I'll operate on you as soon as I can arrange it."

She gave him a questioning look. "Is it true you operate only at night?"

He seemed surprised. "Who told you that?"

Not wanting to betray Helen, she said quickly, "Lisa. When she was here the other night."

He looked angry. "Lisa talks far too much!"

"Is there anything wrong with my knowing about it?"

"No," he said, in a taut voice. "Only I like to give these details to the patients personally at the time I decide. I don't want facts dribbled out as gossip."

"I'm sorry," she said. "But you do operate at night then?"

"Yes. I find it the most suitable time. Many of my clients prefer it."

"But most surgeons operate in the morning, don't they? I mean, that is the accepted medical practice?"

He answered arrogantly. "I do not follow the orthodox rules of my profession," he said. "I have had the courage to devise an entirely new surgical procedure and I conduct this clinic in my own way. Do you understand?"

She was embarrassed and hurt. "I didn't mean to question your ability."

He at once changed his tone. "Forgive my anger. I should have known that."

"I should have expressed myself better," she said.

"And I must remember that we are friends," he said with a return of his former charm. "Now that you are my patient it sometimes escapes me."

"Did you operate last night?"

He nodded. "Yes. I had two patients. The results look most satisfactory."

She was glad to hear the news. It meant that Helen had come through her surgery without mishap. She said, "You must derive a lot of satisfaction from this work of yours."

Dr. Spivak smiled. "It is flattering to have patients seek me out from the very ends of the earth. I am the only one who can offer them hope." ·

"I'm looking forward to a new kind of life after the operation," she said. "And I'll have you to thank for it."

The suave doctor said, "I am more than repaid in having had the pleasure of knowing you."

When he moved on to make the rest of the rounds of the clinic, she sat on the bed thinking about all that he had said. She should have been flattered but she was more worried than anything else. A remembrance of the warnings Douglas had given her over the long-distance phone had come back to haunt her as she wrote the letter to him. There was a small nagging doubt in the back of her mind about whether she was doing the right thing. But she knew she had gone too far. There was no turning back now.

What irked her more than anything else was being kept confined to her room. So she decided after a few days and nights to risk the doctor's anger by wandering a little in the shadowed corridors. For the most part it was easy enough to hide at the sound of anyone's approach. And she was anxious to get a better look around the entire clinic.

On her first expedition in the seemingly endless winding corridors she had a weird experience. She moved out of the wing in which her room was located and went to the adjoining area of the main castle. Here the corridors were wider and the ceilings entirely lost in shadow. She made her way down the length of the impressive corridor when a door suddenly opened ahead of her on the left.

With her heart pounding in fear she pressed herself at once against the wall of a small alove that luckily happened to be near. From this hiding place she was able to watch up the corridor. Through the opened door came Lisa. She was wearing the same elegant old-fashioned gown which she'd been wearing the night of her visit. And her face had that same odd pallor in contrast to her red lips.

Lisa seemed to float down the corridor, staring straight ahead of her. Her broad velvet skirt hid the movement of her feet and legs so that the floating illusion was accomplished. Then behind her came a bent old man in what might almost be called rags. His clothing was stained and torn, and even from the distance at which Adele was spying on him she could smell the odor of decay about him. He had a long, cruel face with twisted black lips. His head was bald except for stray locks of gray hair around his ears and falling down around his collar.

The old man followed Lisa with a shuffling gait and every so often he coughed in a hollow fashion. He was more like an apparition than a human being and Adele could only wonder where the doctor had found such a strange patient.

Then from out of the shadows by the door of that room there came a third figure, this one more monstrous than the second. He was a massive man with clothing of the nineteenth century and a square, cruel face. He wore a black patch over his left eye and had a long scar down his cheek. His good eye had that strange, burning glitter she'd seen in Lisa's eyes, and he was more than six feet tall, and broad.

The weird trio moved slowly down the shadowed corridor like the distorted figures one might encounter in a dream. They were dressed in the manner of folk ready for a costume ball. But this would have to be a macabre event to have such characters attend it. She was stunned by the sight of the three and wondered what it meant.

Were these patients of the clinic eccentric to the point of madness? Was that why they dressed in this fashion and moved silently about the old castle at night? As she stood there hidden in the alcove long after they had passed her, she tried to sort out her impressions of them. And she knew that they had filled her with a kind of terror. The sort of dread she'd known previously when exposed to some mad person. It made her more certain that Dr. Spivak had some mental cases among his patients.

Why hadn't he confided this to her? It would have gone a long way explaining why he was so concerned about the patients wandering freely about the clinic. Because some of those he was treating were insane, he had to conduct the place along the lines of a mental hospital. In a way she was relieved since it explained a good many things for her.

But in another way she found herself more tense. The idea of sharing the clinic with the insane was not too pleasing. And she had been horrified by the appearance of the trio so near to her. She would not want to meet them at such close range soon again.

Taking a deep breath, she left the sanctuary of the alcove to return to her own room. All at once the journey seemed a long and hazardous one. She hated herself for being so jittery but she couldn't help it. The sight of those three heading somewhere in the ancient house for who knew what sort of rendezvous had thoroughly shaken her.

She left the main section of the castle and started down the hallway toward her own room. Then from the shadows there appeared a figure in a long flowing white gown. She halted, not knowing who it could be. And it wasn't until the weird creature came closer to her that she recognized her as Helen, the American girl. But a Helen with a white, blank face and wild staring eyes who bore no resemblance to the vivacious teenager she'd chatted with so cozily a few days before.

CHAPTER 3

"Helen!" she cried in dismay. "What has happened to you?"

The American girl halted and stared at her blankly, showing no hint of recognition. Her throat was heavily bandaged and there was a haggard look about her that was new. She seemed to be in some kind of trance. Slowly she raised a hand and reached out toward Adele in groping fashion.

But before Adele could respond, the harsh voice of Nurse Chisholm sounded from behind her in the corridor. "What's going on here?"

Adele turned to her. "Helen! She seems ill! Did something go wrong with the operation?"

Nurse Chisholm came sternly up to them and took the girl in the flowing white robe by the arm. "You come along with me, my dear," she said in a more subdued voice. And shooting a glance at Adele, she added, "And you go straight to your room where you belong. I'll be in to talk with you in a few minutes."

Adele stood there stunned as the nurse led Helen off down the corridor into the darkness. Something was wrong with the formerly vivacious girl. Very wrong! And it must have to do with the surgery Dr. Spivak had performed on her. Coming after her encounter with the other eerie three, Adele found this a shattering experience.

She returned to her own room and sat on the edge of the bed. She was still seated there when Nurse Chisholm came in to her. She had never been able to correctly understand the gaunt-faced nurse. There were moments when she was considerate and very human, others when she became granite cold and unbending.

She appeared to be in one of her more reasonable moods at this moment. She said, "You know you were breaking a house rule by wandering out there."

"I can't stay in this room endlessly," she protested.

"I'm sorry if it bothers you. But we have reasons for insisting on it."

Adele stood up. "I think I know why."

"You do?" Nurse Chisholm sounded wary.

"Yes. Some of your patients here are mad. I saw three of them in the corridor a little while ago. Lisa and two strange-looking men dressed in the outlandish styles of years ago."

Nurse Chisholm sighed. "You are right. Some of our patients are not normal. That is why we must be so careful."

"But what about Helen? She's changed terribly since her operation. What has happened?"

"She's not recovered from her surgery yet," the nurse said. "She's still in shock. And she is being given sedation. That is why she didn't recognize you or attempt to speak. In a few days she will be perfectly all right once again."

Adele felt a surge of relief. "I'm glad," she said. "I was so worried about her."

"Her operation was a complete success," Nurse Chisholm said. "If you are so apprehensive about the clinic, why did you come here? And why have you remained?"

"I have complete confidence in Dr. Spivak. It's just that the atmosphere here is so strange."

"It is a clinic and not a hotel," the nurse said.

"Of course."

"And you cannot expect to go through surgery without some strain. If you want the benefits you must suffer the ordeal," Nurse Chisholm went on.

"I understand that," she said. "I'd like to talk to Dr. Spivak when I can. You said he has gone to Paris."

"He will return tomorrow. I'll tell him you wish to see him," Nurse Chisholm said. "It will be safer for you if you remain in your room, especially at night."

"I'll remember that," she promised quietly.

Nurse Chisholm went on her way and she was alone in the room again. She felt better knowing that Helen wasn't really suffering from any permanent damage following the operation. She'd merely gotten up from her bed to wander about the corridors before she'd recovered.

Adele read for a little and then went to bed. She had no idea how long she'd slept before she was awakened by a shrill, blood-curdling scream from outside. It brought her awake with a start. And she was so upset by it she left her bed to cross to the tiny window set high in the stone wall of the room to try and look out. Raising herself a little with her hands on the cold sill of the window, she gazed out into the snow-covered courtyard with frightened eyes.

She saw what looked like a dark shadow move by the archway and then it was lost to her. With a troubled expression on her pretty face she left the window to return to bed. But the frightening scream still rang in her ears. It was a long while before she slept. And when she did finally sleep, she had terrible nightmares. One in fact caused her to scream out—bringing Nurse Chisholm to her room. Adele told the English nurse she must speak with Dr. Spivak and Nurse Chisholm promised to let her know when he returned from Paris.

When Nurse Chisholm came with her breakfast tray the stern woman said, "Doctor Spivak returned early this morning."

"Good," Adele said.

There was an odd look on Nurse Chisholm's gaunt face. "Something very unfortunate happened here during the night."

Adele stared at her. "I heard a scream from outside."

"You probably did."

"What was it?"

"Nicholas, the boy who brought us the mail from the village and did odd jobs, was found dead near the archway this morning."

A chill went through her. "I must have heard his death cry. What happened?"

"I don't know. He was attacked by some animal. You can ask the doctor when he comes to see you," the nurse said and quickly left.

The news of the pleasant youth's death had shocked her. She listlessly ate the plain breakfast provided by the hospital and was just finishing her tea when Dr. Spivak arrived.

He was as suave as ever in his white smock as he stood staring at her with those hypnotic eyes and said, "I understand you have been unhappy during my short absence."

She was on her feet facing him. "I become bored being alone in this room so much."

"It is the clinic rule."

"I know."

"Well, we won't dwell on that," he said easily. "Some unfortunate things have been going on while I was in Paris. Helen got up from her bed while still under sedation and could have done herself great harm. I believe you saw her."

"Yes. She's all right now, is she?"

"Doing very well," he said. "And then the youth who did various errands for us, Nicholas, was found dead by the archway this morning. Most unfortunate! The villagers are badly upset by it."

"What happened?"

Those strange glittering eyes met hers. "He was attacked by some animal. The marks are clearly visible on his throat."

Her eyes widened. "What sort of animal?"

He shrugged. "Who knows? Some mountain beast."

"Will you try and track it down?" she asked.

"Unfortunately, there was a snowfall between midnight and dawn. And apparently after the murder. So there are no tracks to give a clue as to the nature of the beast or where it went afterward."

"That's too bad," she said.

He sighed. "Yes. These things are frightening. So you will understand why I try to give my patients every protection. It is for your own good."

"I'm sorry to have been a trouble," she said.

Dr. Stefan Spivak smiled. "You mustn't worry about it. And I have good news for you. I will be able to schedule your operation tonight. So the long tiring period of this business will be over and done with."

His announcement had a strange effect on her: she was both glad and sorry. It would be good to have the suspense ended, but now she found herself worried about what she might undergo.

She said, "You're sure it will turn out all right?"

"You'll thank me all over again when it is finished," he said. "We will operate around seven. Nurse Chisholm will bring you sedation in the late afternoon. And you will take no more food for the balance of the day."

"I have never seen the surgery," she said.

"Let me show it to you after you have recovered," the suave doctor said. "Now you might find it frightening. It is very modern and well-equipped. And it is in the attic of the castle and reached by a smooth-working elevator. Our recovery room is also on that floor."

She gave him a rueful look. "Now that the moment has

arrived, I'm afraid."

He patted her arm. "Natural. But think of the successful operations I've performed and what this will mean to you."

"Yes. I won't be really ill for more than a few days, will I?"

"You're in perfect health. It could be less than that. But I want you to remain here for a week or two afterward to undergo tests, and so I can be sure you are going to benefit by the surgery."

"My fiance was all against this."

"Because he doesn't understand my work," Dr. Stefan Spivak said. "I would gladly have you driven to Zurich to take the afternoon plane back to London, but I know you'd regret it the moment you left here. You'd be coming back later asking for my help and I might then be too busy to offer it. In the summer tourist season there is a vastly larger number seeking help here."

She nodded. "I know. I intend to go through with it."

He smiled. "Excellent. Try not to worry. I want you in the best of shape for the operating table."

But when he left her she did worry. The sight of the haggard-looking Helen had upset her. And despite the insistence of both the doctor and nurse that the girl looked and acted strangely only because she'd wandered about in a state of sedation, she couldn't erase from her mind the memory of those wild, staring eyes.

She would go through the same difficult state of convalescence. Was it worth it? Had Douglas been right in trying to dissuade her from the operation? Perhaps. But as Dr. Spivak had pointed out, Douglas was entirely unfamiliar with this type of surgery and its beneficial results.

The hours edged by. She became almost ill with hunger. But Dr. Spivak had said she was to have no food. Finally Nurse Chisholm arrived with a small glass of colorless liquid on a tray. The nurse's expression was even more grim than usual.

"Take this while I'm here," she said curtly.

"Is it pleasant? I feel rather ill. I'm afraid it might upset my stomach," Adele worried, the small glass in her hand.

"It is tasteless and it will quiet your stomach," Nurse Chisholm said as she stood there watching her.

"Very well." She drank the stuff. It was tasteless. Then she gave the glass back to the nurse. "When will it begin to work?"

"Within a few minutes," Nurse Chisholm said. "And it's action will grow stronger as time passes. You will do best if you stretch out on the bed."

"It is that strong?"

"It's the only pre-medication you'll be given until you are

taken to surgery," Nurse Chisholm told her.

Though she still felt completely normal, she rested on the bed. The grim nurse placed a blanket over her. And suddenly the full impact of the drug hit her. Nurse Chisholm's face became blurred as it hovered above her and there was a strange ringing in her ears. She slipped into a relaxed mindless state and remained in it.

She had no idea how much time had passed. But she saw that Nurse Chisholm and Dr. Spivak had come into the room and were discussing her as they stood at the foot of her bed. Their figures seemed strangely elongated and their faces floated high above her. She decided she wanted to ask them why they looked so strange, but when she tried to speak no words would come.

Then two nurses came with a stretcher on wheels. She was lifted from the bed onto the stretcher and began a journey through long corridors, endless corridors. She closed her eyes, feeling too weary to be bothered by any of it. Until suddenly a bright light glowed above her. And she saw the masked faces of the surgeon and several nurses looking down at her.

She turned her head a little and saw there was another light and another operating table to the left of the one she was on. And stretched out on this table with a white sheet draped over her body was Lisa! What was this Lisa doing here in the operating room with her?

"Ready," she heard Dr. Spivak's harsh voice.

One of the nurses roughly moved Adele's head so she could not see Lisa any longer. She tormented her drugged brain in an effort to recall what Lisa had said that night about the opposites? It was necessary to have an opposite, or what was it? She couldn't think! Her brain was too numbed. And then to end any attempt to understand what was going on, a mask was clamped over her face. A sweet odor filled the small dark world into which she had descended. And almost at once she blacked out.

When she opened her eyes again her throat was aching and her vision blurred. Gradually she focused her eyes and saw that she was in a tiny white-walled room with subdued fighting. And the hospital bed she was in had high runged barriers around it like a crib. She felt very weak and confused. It took her a few minutes to realize she'd been operated on and this must be the recovery room.

Then the door from the corridor opened and Dr. Stefan Spivak came in. He was wearing his white smock and he crossed to the bed and gazed down at her with professional interest.

"You have come out of it well," he told her.

She fixed her gaze on his hawk-face. "How long?"

"You've been unconscious for two days," he told her. "But that is all over. It will be a steady improvement now you've passed the crisis. I'd expect you to be up and walking in three or four days."

"I feel so weak and ill," she said worriedly.

"You can expect to for at least another twenty-four hours," he said. "I will be giving you nightly transfusions of blood for several weeks. That is part of the treatment and will add to your strength."

She frowned. "I don't recall your mentioning the transfusions before."

"I'm sure I must have," he said smiling suavely.

Her memory was returning and now she asked, "What was Lisa doing on that other operating table beside me?"

His eyebrows raised. "Lisa?"

"Yes."

He smiled coldly. "You must have imagined that. A drug delirium on your part. I can promise you Lisa was not in the operating room. There was no one on that other operating table."

"But I saw her plainly," she protested.

"Sometimes illusions of that sort are more real than reality," the doctor said. "Now you mustn't talk any longer. I'm going to give you an injection that will make you sleep again."

With frightened eyes she saw him prepare the needle she didn't want. But she was too weak and ill to offer any objections. She knew that he was lying to her and that she had seen Lisa on that other table. She made up her mind she'd find out the truth about it when she was feeling better. The long needle of the hypodermic gleamed in the light as he brought it down close to her arm. She felt the sting of its entry into her flesh and the surge of whatever it contained into her veins.

"There we are," he said in a satisfied tone as he drew away the hypodermic. "Now you'll sleep."

And she did. She had no idea how long. But when she opened her eyes again she felt much better. She was able to sit up in bed. It was night once more and she suspected she had slept around the clock.

Nurse Chisholm came into the room and gave her a sharp look. "I see you're awake."

"Yes. I feel greatly improved."

"It's about time," the nurse said. "Now I'll attend to your transfusion. After you have it you can get up and walk around the room if you want to."

Adele stared at her. "Why do I need this transfusion? I feel all right."

"Doctor's orders. To give you strength."

The nurse went about setting up the transfusion bottle and within a short time the red blood from the glass container was dripping into a vein of her arm. She was upset because she felt she didn't require it and determined to take this up with Dr. Spivak as soon as he appeared. But as the bottle emptied she realized that almost immediately she had gained surprising strength. And oddly she felt no desire for food or drink.

She told Nurse Chisholm this, saying, "I'm neither hungry nor thirsty. And it seems I should be."

The nurse looked grim. "The doctor purposely doesn't want you to put anything in your stomach for a while. That's why he's giving you the transfusions."

This seemed odd to her, but she couldn't argue that the doctor was wrong. She did feel very well. After the transfusion she got out of bed and moved about the room. A kind of elation thrilled through her, a well-being she didn't understand. She stood by the window and gazed out at the stars in the dark sky and the snow-capped mountains outlined against this background.

Turning to Nurse Chisholm she said, "I've never realized how much I love the night. I have the feeling I prefer it to day anytime."

Nurse Chisholm eyed her uneasily. "That's just as well since it's the night you'll be seeing from now on."

Startled, she asked, "What do you mean?"

The grim-faced nurse said, "Doctor Spivak insists that after the operation his patients sleep by day and have their activity at night. It is part of his therapy."

She listened thoughtfully. "I believe he did mention that."

"So at dawn you return to sleep," Nurse Chisholm said. "And you will not open your eyes again until dusk."

"I won't mind," Adele said. "It sounds like a pleasant change of routine."

"You'll get used to it," the older woman said dryly.

Adele touched a hand to her cheek. "I must look a sight."

She glanced around. "And I don't see a single mirror in the room? Do you happen to have a small one?"

"No," the nurse said sharply. "You've had enough excitement for a start. You can wait to look into a mirror later. You're still pretty enough, so don't fret."

Adele had no choice but to return to the hospital bed. But she was unable to sleep so she read for a little and listened to a small short-wave radio the nurse brought her. It was dawn before she yawned and sank back on the bed to sleep.

Dusk was settling when she sat up in bed again and stretched. She felt refreshed and a good deal like her former self. Her throat no longer ached and she was anxious to leave the hospital recovery room and return to her own room on the lower floor. A few minutes later Nurse Chisholm bustled in and prepared the transfusion apparatus.

"I don't need blood again!" Adele protested as the nurse connected the bottle of blood to her arm.

Nurse Chisholm gave her a disgusted look. "That's what you think!"

"I'll complain to Dr. Spivak," she said.

"Do that," Nurse Chisholm said as she finished with the transfusion set-up and left the room.

She impatiently waited for the blood to transfer into her vein. It made her feel even better but she considered it nonsense. By the time the blood was half gone. Dr. Spivak came in with a look of interest on his hawk face.

"Having your nightly supply of blood," he said.

"I don't need it," she protested.

His hypnotic eyes met hers. "It may surprise you to hear that you do need it badly. Without it you'd soon be in great torment."

"Only because I'm not eating or drinking," she said. "I'd rather begin to have my meals regularly."

"I'm afraid that's not possible yet," Dr. Spivak told her.

"When can I return to my room?"

"Tomorrow evening, perhaps."

"Can't I go down in the morning?"

"Not after dawn comes," Dr. Spivak said. "You must sleep then."

"It's a weird routine."

"Perhaps. But you have to adapt yourself to it until you are fully well again."

She asked, "And when I leave your clinic?"

He shrugged. "You may find it more convenient to go on living as a night person. Once you are out of the hospital I leave the choice to you."

"I see," she said. "Well, it shouldn't be a difficult one. I'll likely go back to my former style of living. I enjoy the nights, but then so much happens during the days."

Dr. Spivak seemed amused. "I promise that you will be startled to learn how much of your life will take on importance at night from now on."

"You talk rather strangely," she said. "I'm not sure I

understand."

"You will, later. Don't worry about it now," he said.

"Where is Helen?" She suddenly remembered the American girl. "Is she fully recovered?"

"Helen?" he sounded puzzled.

"You know," she insisted. "You operated on her and she was to work as your secretary in return for the surgery."

"Oh, yes," he said. "I'd forgotten. She's not here any longer."

"Not here?"

"No," he said, smiling wryly. "She wanted to leave and I decided not to hold her to her bargain. She was very upset by the death of that boy, Nicholas. It seems they had become friends. So she left here altogether."

Adele felt let down. "I'm disappointed. I wanted so much to talk to her again."

"Who knows?" the doctor said. "Maybe you two will meet somewhere."

"It's hardly likely," Adele sighed.

"You mustn't try to rush things," Dr. Stefan Spivak said with one of his suave smiles. "Obey Nurse Chisholm, get plenty of rest and try not to worry your brain with useless questions. Do all that and you'll recover in no time at all."

Adele followed his instructions and two weeks went by with a general improvement on her part. She slept each day, had her regular evening blood transfusion and read or wandered about outside during most of the night. She was still restricted to a certain area of the castle-like clinic and Dr. Spivak had installed a new grilled iron door at the entrance to the main building from her wing. This was always kept locked.

She resented this but comforted herself with long night walks in the nearby countryside. On one of these nocturnal occasions she stumbled upon a hilly graveyard. She was fascinated by the old cemetery and moved about its snow-covered graves and worn tombstones with delight. Almost every night she went there. It was hard to explain the attraction it held for her, but somehow she felt at home there.

Then it was time for Douglas Edwards to come and meet her. Dr. Spivak was away on one of his many trips when her fiance arrived. She left word with Nurse Chisholm that she would meet the young man the first night of his stay in the village. And when she awoke from her day's sleep the grim-faced nurse told her that Douglas would be coming by for her in a car at seven to take her to the village inn for dinner.

Nurse Chisholm brought out the transfusion equipment

and warned her, "We must hurry and give you your transfusion first."

"No," Adele protested, "I feel well enough. It will take too long. I want to take time with dressing and make-up and look my best when my fiance gets here."

The grim nurse stood with the container of blood in her hand. "You need this."

"Not tonight. You can give it to me tomorrow evening." A strange look crossed Nurse Chisholm's dour face. "You may be sorry you refused to listen to me."

"I'll take that chance," Adele said with a touch of anger. "I'm about to be discharged as a patient here and I'm sick of being restricted and ordered about."

"Very well, Miss," Nurse Chisholm said with unexpected quietness and she put the equipment away and left the room.

Adele sat down at the dresser to make herself up and realized she still had no mirror in the room. She looked in her handbag and the mirror in it had vanished. Upset, she tried to locate Nurse Chisholm but couldn't find her. She was sure the dour woman was keeping out of the way to punish her for refusing the transfusion. And she was forced to use a simple make-up that she could risk without being able to check it in a looking glass of some type.

She also realized for the first time that lately she'd not been wearing her own clothes but a dress provided by the clinic, one of dark velvet similar to the one she'd seen so often on Lisa. Remembrance of Lisa made her wonder what had happened to the strange girl. And what had become of her eerie, mad companions?

She wore a warm red pants suit and her leather sports coat and was ready when Douglas drove his small sports car into the courtyard. When he got out to meet her there was an anxious look on his thin face. He was hatless and wore a short dark coat with a gray scarf wound around his neck. As she came to meet him in the courtyard, he took her in his arms and smiled.

"Good to see you," he said. And he kissed her. "Your lips are ice cold."

"No wonder. The clinic isn't too well heated," she said. He gave the big gray building an apprehensive look. "I'll be glad to have you out of there. I've worried the whole time."

She smiled. "There was no need. I'm very well."

Douglas was staring at her. "You're thin. But that's to be expected, I suppose."

Douglas helped her in the car and they began the drive along the snow-covered road to the village below. At the wheel, he said, "The food at the inn is good. You'll enjoy your dinner tonight."

Adele made no immediate reply as she sat there in a kind of tense state. The thought of food or drink sickened her. Worse than that, she realized she had made a bad error in not taking the transfusion. She felt weak and restless. And as the car drove by the ancient cemetery where she so often wandered at night, she knew that what was bothering her was a craving for blood!

CHAPTER 4

The dining room of the inn was warm and noisy with music and the conversation of the people at the many tables. Though Douglas had arranged for a table in a shadowed corner of the room, Adele felt stifled and afraid. The crowd in the room pressed in on her. And the heat was unbearable after she had grown accustomed to the cold of the clinic for so long.

After the hearty meal Douglas had ordered was served, he stared at her with worried eyes and asked, "Are you feeling ill? You look deathly pale."

"It's the heat," she murmured. "And so many people. They bother me."

Douglas looked startled. "This is not a large place. There aren't many people here. You always loved the big London restaurants."

"Perhaps it's because I'm still rather weak," she said, toying with her fork. She'd not been able to eat or drink anything as yet.

"You should never have gone through with that operation," the young man said angrily.

"It's done with," she told him. "I don't want to talk about it."

"I warned you against it," Douglas said, not heeding her wish to end the argument.

Her eyes fixed on him. "It is my life. I have a right to do what

I like with it."

"Throw it away to a quack?" was his angry demand.

"I'm sure the operation was a success."

"I wish I could be," he told her. "You look a wreck. And you're not eating any of your dinner!"

"I don't feel like it," she said. "And as soon as you've finished your meal, I'd appreciate your driving me back to the clinic."

Douglas was distressed. "This is some awful reunion," he told her.

It had been a disappointing evening. She was only too aware of that. On the drive back through the wintery night, she tried to keep up some kind of conversation with him, but her tense state made it impossible. For the last third of the drive back she sat in silence, overwhelmed by her craving for blood. She knew this could be the end of their engagement and she didn't care.

At last he drove under the arch into the courtyard of the gray old castle. There were few lights at its tiny windows, and everything was somber and silent.

He frowned. "This place is like a house of the dead. It's deserted."

"Doctor Spivak likes to have it very quiet."

"He's certainly succeeded," the young man said with disgust.

"He is against publicity," Adele said nervously. "Now I must go in."

"When will I see you again?"

"I don't know whether we should meet again," she said.

He looked alarmed. "Adele! Don't talk that way. We're supposed to go back to London together. Or have you fallen in love with this mysterious doctor?"

"Don't bother me with endless questions," she protested.

"Adele!" he said brokenly and took her in his arms to kiss her again.

She submitted to the kiss but made it a brief one. Then as she was about to draw back, the overpowering compulsion took control of her. And in the next second she touched her lips to his throat as if to kiss him. But this was to be more than a kiss. Her teeth sank into his flesh so that she knew the sweet taste of blood. She heard his soft moan but paid no attention to it. Instead she went on taking blood from him until her needs were satiated.

When she finally drew away from him, he slumped over the wheel unconscious. Horrified by what she had done, she flung open the car door and quickly escaped into the clinic. She ran down the gloomy corridor to her room, and when she was inside she threw herself on the bed and wept.

She lay there for perhaps twenty minutes before she regained control of herself and began to worry about Douglas. She got up and went to the window and saw that he had emerged from his faint and was standing by his car, staring at the castle door. She was afraid he might try to rouse Nurse Chisholm or some of the others and she felt she must send him on his way to the village. So she forced herself to go out to him.

She descended the steps of the castle and crossed the snow-covered courtyard to confront him in the moonlight. She saw that he was pale and shaken.

"I'm sorry, Adele," he said. "I don't know what happened after we kissed. I sort of fainted. I must have been drinking too much."

"It's all right," she said, relieved to know that he recalled nothing of her attack. It was seemingly a blank in his memory.

"I feel weak and dizzy-headed," he said.

"Are you able to drive?"

"Yes. My head is clearing slowly."

"Then go back to the village," she told him. "It can be dangerous in the countryside at night."

He nodded, his eyes anxious. "When will we start back to London?"

"I want you to go home tomorrow. Alone."

"Alone?"

"I'm sorry, Douglas," she said. "Don't ask me to explain. Perhaps I'll see you in London. Now go and don't try to argue."

"Adele!" he pleaded.

"I won't change my mind," she said. And she turned and went back into the old castle.

By the time she reached her room and looked out the window, his car had gone. The courtyard was empty. She wouldn't see Douglas again. The desolation and fear this brought her filled her eyes with tears. She had sent him away for his own good. She knew something dreadful had happened to her. She felt she might be insane. The operation had gone wrong in some way! If only Dr. Spivak would come back so she could explain to him.

She paced the room restlessly until dawn came and sleep overtook her. And she slept through the next day like one of the dead. At dusk she wakened and found Nurse Chisholm standing by her bedside.

Nurse Chisholm gave her a wise look. "Do you want your transfusion tonight?"

She sat up in bed. "Yes," she said quietly. "I will take it."

As the dour nurse busied herself with the preparations for the treatment, she said, "How did you make out with your young man last night?"

"He's going back to London alone."

"Oh?"

"Yes," she said. "I decided I wasn't well enough to go with him. I must remain here and discuss my case with Doctor Spivak. When will he get back?"

"I couldn't say," Nurse Chisholm said in her expressionless way as she made ready to thrust the transfusion needle into Adele's arm.

Adele winced at the needle's sting. Then worriedly, she asked, "When his operations have gone wrong, what has happened to the patients?"

Nurse Chisholm looked wary. "Few of Doctor Spivak's surgical cases are failures."

"Some of them must be!"

"In most cases of failure the patients have died."

Her eyes questioned the nurse. "Did any of them become insane?"

Nurse Chisholm hesitated; then she said, "I'm not qualified to discuss such things. You'll have to wait and ask the doctor." And she left her.

But there had been a revelation in the wariness and evasion of Nurse Chisholm's reply which left Adele in no doubt. There had been such failures. And surely the weird-looking men she'd seen in the main wing of the clinic with Lisa that night had been examples. And now the main wing was locked to her, undoubtedly to keep her from discovering more truths about what was going on in the old stone castle.

The transfusion made her feel relaxed and normal. Nurse Chisholm returned to put the equipment away. With a glance of concern the dour woman said, "You will soon have to be making plans to leave. Doctor Spivak doesn't like patients remaining here too long after their operations."

"I will leave," she said. "But I want to talk to him first."

Nurse Chisholm went away again and Adele was left in the lonely room to brood over her plight. After a while she decided to go for a walk. So she put on her coat and overshoes and the scarf she wrapped around her head and throat and made her way to the door leading to the courtyard. It was a clear, cold night and she walked briskly across the snow. At last she came to the cemetery and felt a wave of comfort go through her. It was as if she were among friends!

She strolled along the frozen paths between the graves, pausing every now and then before a weathered gravestone. Then she noticed she was not alone in the place of the dead. A distance away from her and with his back to her was the massive mad man with the patch over his eye whom she'd seen at the clinic. She could tell it was him by his tall figure and broad shoulders. She dodged behind a gravestone to watch him with frightened eyes.

He had been standing before a tombstone and now he moved on toward the cemetery exit. She let him get a distance ahead of her before she started after him. His massive hulk stood out against the snow and she had no difficulty trailing him to another door of the castle outside the courtyard. He entered the big oaken door. She waited in the shadow of a tree and then after a moment followed him.

Once through the doorway, she found herself in a part of the clinic she had never visited before. The foyer was more elegant than in her wing and the corridors leading from it wider. She stood there in the shadows trying to get her bearings and decide which corridor she should take. Then she heard a burst of old-fashioned music. A string orchestra was playing what sounded to her like a stately minuet.

Attracted by the music, she took the corridor from which the sound came. The corridor was dark, but light streamed from the double doors of the room in which the music was being played. And now she could hear a babble of voices in excited conversation and occasional laughter. It sounded like a huge party! Perhaps a costume ball?

And when she came near enough to the door to see in, she discovered this to be actually what was going on. A costume ball! The members of the orchestra wore ancient knee britches and white wigs and played on a platform backed by giant mirrors at the end of the great ballroom. And couples were grouped all around the walls of the room watching a group of perhaps a dozen go through the pattern of the minuet. All of them were wearing clothes of another day! It was like a phantom nightmare from the past. Unreal!

Then she studied the mirrors and saw that not a single person in the room was reflected in the wall of glass, not a musician, none of the watchers and none of the dancers. It was as if they didn't exist. As if the room were empty!

Fear shot through her and she turned and ran down the hall in an effort to get as far away from the ghostly figures as she could. And all at once she came to a table with a candelabra on it and lighted candles and a large mirror above it. She hesitated to get a glimpse of herself in this, the first mirror she'd come upon in weeks, and it was then she had the ultimate experience of horror! Her reflection showed no more in this mirror than the reflections of those other weird creatures in the ballroom. She was one of them!

She turned from the mirror with terror distorting her pretty face and found herself confronted by the dour nurse. At the sight of the grim woman, she gasped and drew back.

Nurse Chisholm said sharply, "You know you have no right in this part of the clinic."

Crouching in the darkness, Adele asked in a low, taut voice, "What have you done to me?"

Nurse Chisholm looked uneasy. "I don't know what you're talking about."

She stared at her with terrified eyes. "Yes, you do!"

"Let me take you back to your room," Nurse Chisholm said and moved close to grasp her by the arm.

"No!" Adele screamed. And she tore herself loose of the woman's grip as at the same time she grasped her by the shoulders and then lunged forward to touch her lips to the nurse's throat.

It was now the middle-aged nurse's turn to cry out in terror. "No! Don't do that! Don't take my blood!"

Adele stared at her frightened face in disgust and horror. "Then it's true," she said. "Your Doctor Spivak has turned me into a vampire! One of the walking dead!"

The nurse was terrified. "I didn't have any part in it!"

"I know too well the part you played," was her grim reply. "And I shall drain every drop of blood from your body if you don't tell me the truth about what I'm going to ask."

"You can trust me," Nurse Chisholm insisted.

"What is going on in this place?"

"Just what the doctor said. Pituitary transplants, but for reasons different than he told you. He gets opposites to donate part of their pituitary glands to his wealthy patients who are vampires. The transplant cures them for at least a few years. They come from everywhere to have him help them. Some of them have lived as vampires for hundreds of years."

Adele's fiercely gripping hands cut into the shoulder bones of the terrified nurse. Softly Adele said, "So you stole part of my healthy pituitary to save one of them. And at the same time turned me into a vampire."

"Don't blame me!" the nurse protested. "I tried to warn you."

"Not properly," Adele said. "What can I do to get away from here and live a normal life?"

"You can never do that," the nurse said in a quavering voice.

"There must be someone I can turn to for help," she said.

"Only one," the frightened nurse gasped. "His name is Barnabas Collins and he lives in London. He knows about Doctor Spivak and hates him."

"Barnabas Collins," she repeated the name.

"He lives at number twenty Kent Square in London," Nurse Chisholm said. "And if you're wise, you'll go there now. Before Doctor Spivak gets back. I can only warn you again."

"What other harm can he do me?" Adele asked bitterly.

"More than you think!" the nurse warned her. "He likes to experiment and he could insist on a second operation. And that one would really leave you a harmless vegetable. Consider yourself lucky to be as bright as you are!"

The woman's words brought new fear to her. "How can I leave here?" she demanded. "I can't travel except at night! As a vampire I'm doomed to live only in the hours of darkness. And I must have blood to sustain me."

"Travel by night and sleep between plane trips," was Nurse Chisholm's advice. "Walk to the village and hire a car from there to Zurich. There are two or three night flights to London. You can find Barnabas Collins before morning!"

"What will you tell Doctor Spivak?" she demanded. The woman's dour face was white and her eyes bulged with fear. "I'll say that you ran off to the village and I didn't know until it was too late to stop you."

"Where is Lisa?"

"The Countess Dario? She's already away from here. The doctor cured her."

"By using me," Adele said bitterly. "And Helen?"

"She's become like you. A poor lost soul! He gave her the choice of a second operation or going on her way. She vanished a few nights ago! You'd be wise to follow her!"

Adele relinquished her hold on the older woman and saw Nurse Chisholm fall to her knees. "How can I believe you about this Barnabas Collins? How can I know he exists or will help me?"

"He will! I swear it! I've sent a few to him before—it's my way of making up for what I'm doing here!"

"You might well try to make up for your actions," Adele said with contempt.

Nurse Chisholm got to her feet awkwardly. "I have to stay here and work for him. I can't go back to England. The police want me!"

"That doesn't surprise me," Adele said. "Now take me to my room and help me prepare for the trip."

The grim-faced woman led her along several other dark corridors until they came to the grilled iron door. She unlocked it and they went into the section of the clinic familiar to Adele. When they reached her room, the nurse helped her pack.

And then she was stepping out into the cold with a frightened Nurse Chisholm standing in the doorway to see her off. "Remember I'm not all bad!" the nurse called after her. "I'm giving you a chance to save yourself!"

Adele was already hastening across the courtyard. She didn't stop to look back at the woman or the ghostly gray castle. Her single suitcase in hand, she crossed under the snow-draped archway for what was to be the last time and headed along the path that would eventually take her to the village. When she reached the cemetery she had an overwhelming longing to remain there, but she forced herself to go on. She must fight her way back to the world of the living.

The night winds stung her face and she bent her head against them. The bag she was carrying seemed to grow heavier with every step. But at last she saw the lights of the village and made for the inn where she had visited with Douglas.

Poor Douglas! She had feasted on his blood and then sent him away without telling him the real reason she had rejected him. Perhaps if she was frank with him and told him everything he'd try to help her. But he would help out of pity rather than love and she didn't want that. Better to try and find this Barnabas Collins if there was such a man!

When she reached the door of the inn all the lights were out. She rang the night bell and waited there in the freezing cold. After a long while she heard footsteps from the other side of the door. The light over it was turned on and the door opened a fraction as the elderly inn owner, his bathrobe wrapped around him, peered out at her nervously.

"Yes?" he said.

"I need to hire a car to take me to Zurich," she told him. "It's urgent!"

"It is very late," the old man said. "My son has the taxi. He's asleep."

"I will pay him well," she said pleadingly. "It's a matter of life and death."

The old man studied her through the partly opened door with suspicion. "You're not one of them?"

She felt a surge of despair. "One of whom?" she asked in a tense voice, though she knew well enough what he meant.

"The ones in the castle," the innkeeper said. "They are not for honest folk to mix with. They are all cursed!"

She shook her head. "I'm a tourist. My car broke down a distance from here. I was given a lift this far. Now I must get on to Zurich to catch the night plane for London."

The old man opened the door grudgingly. "Come inside," he said. "I'll have to go upstairs and wake my son." She sat in a wooden chair near the door for ten minutes or so. And then a young man descended the stairs with the innkeeper following him. He was already putting on his overcoat.

He said, "You want to be driven to the Zurich airport?"

"Please," she said tensely. "I don't care what the charge is."

The young man gave her a reproving look. "My father and I don't make it a practice to take advantage of people in distress. The fare will be the regular one. I'll have the car around to pick you up in a few minutes."

Ten minutes later she was relaxing in the rear seat of the over-age limousine which served as the hotel's taxi. She knew that at last she was on her way to freedom.

The young man at the wheel was an experienced driver and genial enough. As they drove along he told her, "You must forgive my father for being gruff with you at the start. We have a strange lot of people in the old castle which is now being operated as a clinic. He was afraid you were one of them."

"I know," she said. "He told me."

"We had a boy working for us, Nicholas. He began doing errands for that Doctor Spivak. Next thing he became friendly with some girl up there. And one night he was attacked by some kind of creature. They found him dead in the morning with his throat punctured as if by fangs. Local folk know what those marks mean. They are the sign of the vampire."

"Do you believe in such things?"

"Yes," he said. "There is great evil going on in that castle. We cannot tolerate it much longer. My father has spoken to the authorities. And soon we hope they will raid the place and rid our village of that menace."

"It's a very strange story," she said, pretending surprise.

"Our mountains are full of mysteries beyond belief," the young man at the wheel assured her as they drove on through the wintery night.

The Zurich airport with its modern buildings and neon lights almost made her believe that all that had happened in that mountain clinic had been a nightmare. That she was still a normal human being. But she knew better. She paid the young man his fare, went into the airport and found she had an hour to spare before the plane left for England. She bought a ticket and sat down to wait. The thing that terrified her was that dawn would break before she reached Barnabas Collins. She opened her handbag and took out the paper on which she'd written his address. After reading it over for perhaps the tenth time, she put it away.

Fortunately the plane left promptly. She was now nervously calculating and believed they should land at the London airport about three in the morning. If she managed to get a taxi straight from the airport no longer than a half-hour later, she should be able to reach Barnabas Collins. It would still be well before dawn. She would tell him her story and beg refuge and help from him. And unless Nurse Chisholm had lied to her, she would find a friend in this stranger.

The plane trip to London was uneventful. She had her passport and was able to get through customs without any delay. It was busy at the airport even at this hour of the morning, and she had to wait for a little before finding a taxi. Then she gave the driver the Kent Square address.

He was a small man with a wizened face and he eyed her solemnly. "You want to go there at this time of night?"

"Why not?"

"The address isn't as good as it sounds, Miss. It's in Soho. Better to go to a hotel and find this place in the morning."

She shook her head. "No. I prefer to go straight there now."

The little man shrugged. "Whatever you say, Miss."

Just being back on English soil gave her confidence. Somehow she would save herself from the terrible thing Dr. Spivak had done to her. She must try to battle the evil his surgeon's knife had implanted in her and survive as a normal human being. But was it possible? Could she even depend on this Barnabas Collins, who apparently lived in the underworld section of London? What sort of person would he be?

The taxi halted before a pub with dim lights showing in its windows. There was an open door leading to a dark stairway next to the pub. The driver turned to her and said, "Up those stairs. That's the number you gave me, Miss."

"Thank you," she said. And she fumbled for the money to pay him.

She stood by the open doorway for a moment as the taxi drove off. A swarthy young man came staggering out of the pub to stare at her and smile drunkenly. She sensed that he was coming to accost her, and before he could do so she quickly went inside and hurried up the black stairway. At the top there was a door and she pounded on it vigorously. At the same time she glanced down the stairs with frightened eyes to be sure the young man wasn't coming up after her. He wasn't.

That crisis avoided, she gave all her attention to waking whoever was in the flat. She knocked loudly again and then heard a complaining female voice and the patter of footsteps. After a moment the door was opened by a short, stout woman in a nightcap and dark dressing gown.

"Well, what's all this row about?" the stout woman asked with a frown on her matronly features.

"I was sent here," she said anxiously. "I'm sorry to arrive at such an unlikely hour. But I need help badly. And I was told that Barnabas Collins could offer it to me and that he lives here."

The woman eyed her suspiciously. "Are you a friend of Mr. Collins?"

"No. But someone told me I could come to him for help."

"I won't deny that, since he's a fine man," the woman said. "But Barnabas Collins isn't here."

"Oh!" she gasped, her spirits falling. She'd known this could happen but prayed that it wouldn't. "When will he be back?"

"I don't know," the woman said. And she eyed her worriedly. "You look fair ill! You'd better come in and have a spot of hot tea or maybe a taste of brandy."

"I'll come in," Adele said. "But I don't want anything except to learn where I can reach Barnabas Collins."

The stout woman showed her into an old-fashioned sitting room and indicated an easy chair for her to sit in. Then the woman said, "I'm sorry, Miss. I can tell you're badly upset. But Mr. Collins has gone to a place called Collinsport in the United States. It is the place where he was born and he returns there regularly."

Tears brimmed in Adele's eyes. "That's dreadful. I must talk to him."

"Collinsport isn't all that far away in these days of plane travel," the old woman said. "Mr. Collins tells me it takes him only nine hours from here to the Portland airport in America, which is not far from the village where he goes. And from that airport it is only a three-hour car trip to his door."

She sat in the leather-covered chair numbed with fear and desperation. Then she told the woman, "The difficulty is I can only travel by night. I must rest during the daytime. And it will soon be dawn."

Understanding showed on the stout woman's round face. "I know, Miss," she said. "We've often had your sort here before. And Mr. Collins has never turned anyone away. So I can't do less, since I'm looking after the place while he is gone. You can stay here until tomorrow night and then begin arranging to travel to Collinsport."

CHAPTER 5

Since Barnabas Collins' housekeeper knew all about the living
dead and the help given them by her employer, she was in no way
terrified of Adele. She gave her a room in which to sleep for the day.
And when night came again she helped with airline schedules so that
Adele was able to board a night flight to Boston.

She barely reached the American city before dawn. And
there was a long ordeal again with the officials there. But finally she
reached the sanctuary of the airport motel and remained there all
the following day. At dusk she got up from her vampire sleep with a
ravenous thirst for blood. She was tense and ill and knew she could
not go on unless she had some.

So she called room service for an order of food. And by a
happy chance it was delivered by a personable young waitress. She
signed the check and gave the girl a tip. And then as the waitress
turned to leave, Adele pounced on her and sank her teeth into her
throat. She felt the warm blood in her mouth and took enough of it
to fill her needs. Then she gently let the unconscious girl down to the
carpeted floor.

She knew it would only be a short time until the girl was
missed. So she quickly put out the lights in the room, picked up her
already packed bag and left. On the way out she paid her bill and
then hurried across to the lobby of the airline serving Maine and

booked passage on a plane leaving for Portland within a half-hour.

The wait in the lobby of the airline tested her nervous strength. At any moment she feared the police would come in looking for her. But luckily nothing like that happened, and she was able to board the plane without interference. At last she felt relatively safe.

The flight to Portland took only thirty minutes. It was now seven-thirty in the evening. And she hired a taxi to take her to Collinsport. Winter in Maine was no less cold or snowy than it had been in Switzerland. And the driver warned her, "There's a snowstorm predicted, Miss. If it comes up along the way I can't promise to get you to Collinsport by ten-thirty."

"Do your best," she said. "Just so long as we get there."

She sat with her eyes closed for much of the drive along the icy roads. It was a very dark night and as they reached the village of Collinsport, the storm finally broke. It began to snow, gently at first and then harder. The taxi driver stopped at a service station and was told the Collins family lived in a great mansion known as Collinwood a distance off the main highway.

By the time the taxi drew up before the entrance of Collinwood a true snowstorm was in progress. Adele paid the taxi driver and allowed him to take her bag to the entrance of Collinwood for her.

As she rang the bell, she asked him, "Will you manage getting back to Portland all right?"

"I'll likely spend the night somewhere along the way," the driver told her. "There are plenty of motels open. I'll go back in the morning." He thanked her for her generous tip and got back into the car and drove off just as the door of Collinwood was opened by a matronly, good-looking woman with dark hair and lovely eyes.

The woman glanced at Adele and her suitcase with some surprise. "Yes?" she said in a low cultured voice.

"My name is Adele Marriot," she said. "And I've just flown over from London. I've come to see Barnabas Collins."

Now the woman smiled as if she understood. "You are a friend of my cousin, Barnabas. I'm Elizabeth Stoddard. Do come in out of the storm."

"Thank you," Adele said gratefully, relieved to have arrived at the right place. "They told the taxi driver that your house was out here. And we saw the lights as we came along the shore road."

"It has become a dreadful stormy night," Elizabeth Stoddard said as she led her into the high-ceilinged foyer of the old mansion. It was dimly lighted and she stopped before a portrait of a handsome, gaunt-faced man which hung on the wall. "Don't you think that portrait resembles Barnabas remarkably?"

Adele hesitated, not wanting to reveal that she'd never even set eyes on Barnabas Collins. She said, "I suppose it does."

"I think so," the matronly woman smiled. "It's actually of an ancestor of his, the first Barnabas Collins."

"Oh?"

"Yes. Cousin Barnabas arrived here from London only a few days ago. Does he expect you?"

"I think not," Adele said hesitantly. "I was in Switzerland when he left England to come here. It will be a sort of surprise."

"Come into the living room for a moment and rest a little," Elizabeth said. "I want you to meet another cousin of Barnabas, my brother, Roger."

Adele was feeling more uneasy every moment. Until she saw Barnabas himself for a private talk, she'd still be in the dark as to whether he could help her. But she felt she must hide her tensions from this woman who was receiving her in such a friendly manner.

The elegant living room had great crystal chandeliers overhead, paneled walnut walls, fine paintings and rich antique furnishings. In a chair before the blazing fireplace at the end of the room sat a stern, middle-aged man with a newspaper in his hands. Hearing them enter, he rose and eyed Adele with a questioning air.

Elizabeth said, "I want you to meet a friend of Barnabas from London, Miss Adele Marriot. My brother, Roger Collins."

Roger nodded with a rather cold expression. "So you are a friend of Cousin Barnabas?"

Adele sensed a stiffness and hostility in the stern-faced man. She said, "I'm looking forward to seeing him."

Roger Collins smiled in a glacial manner. "You realize that you won't meet him here?"

It gave her a nasty shock. "Not find him here?"

Elizabeth spoke up at once, reproaching her brother. "That wasn't very kind of you, Roger." And to Adele she explained, "My brother is right, of course, but he should have explained that Barnabas is living in what we call the old house, which was the original Collinwood. It's on the estate only a very short walk from here."

She felt relief again and warm gratitude for Elizabeth's kindness. "I'm so glad to hear that. It's been a long journey."

Roger Collins, in, a somewhat friendlier tone, asked, "Wouldn't you like to join us with a drink?"

She shook her head. "If you don't mind, no. I'd like to go to Barnabas at once. It's very late and I don't want to keep him up."

Roger laughed at this. "I doubt if you will. He's a regular

night owl. Isn't that so, Elizabeth?"

The dark woman gave Adele a faint smile. "Barnabas does stay up very late, so you needn't be afraid of bursting in on him at this time of night."

"On the contrary," Roger said. "I doubt if you'd find him around during the day."

Adele said, "If you'll tell me the way, I'll go to him at once."

"You can't go alone on this stormy night," Elizabeth said. "Roger will walk there with you."

"It's snowing hard," Roger said. "Why don't you be our guest until tomorrow? Then move on to the old house."

"I appreciate the offer," Adele said. "But I really can't. I'm anxious to speak with your cousin at once on an urgent matter. I've made a very long journey just for that purpose."

"She's right," Elizabeth told her brother. "Put on your clothes and escort her to the old house without delay."

Roger sighed. "Very well. If I must." And he left them to go out and dress for the walk in the storm.

The dark woman turned to her. "You mustn't mind my brother. He is a much nicer person than his manner might indicate. Since I lost my husband he's lived here with me. My daughter and his young son make up our family. You must come and visit with us often while you are here. Carolyn would enjoy meeting you. She's in her late teens but very grown-up and looking forward to some travel."

"I'd like to meet her," Adele said politely.

"David, Roger's son, is younger. But a nice boy. He also prefers the company of adults. I'm afraid the children have led rather isolated lives here."

"It must be lovely in good weather," Adele said. "Your view of the ocean and the quiet here."

Elizabeth's eyes met hers with almost a fearful look in them. "We do enjoy the ocean. But this old house is not as quiet as you might think. Over the years Collinwood has known many strange and sometimes unhappy incidents. But there'll be plenty of time to tell you those things later."

Roger appeared in the doorway of the living room wearing a long, heavy coat and holding a fur hat in his hand. "I'm ready, young woman. The snow is piling up on the ground. And you don't seem to have any overshoes!"

"I'll manage," she said.

"Not in those thin shoes," Elizabeth told her. "I'll let you use an old pair of my overshoes. I'm sure they'll fit." And they did. In a few minutes she left Collinwood and was on her way to the old house with Roger carrying her bag, walking at her side.

The snow was coming down so heavily, she could get no clear idea of what the estate was like. She kept her head bent most of the time, and when she did glance up could see only a few feet before her.

Roger said, "So you are a friend of my cousin's! He is a great one to travel, isn't he?"

"I believe so," she said cautiously.

"No question about it. Never stays long in one place," Roger said. "Now I've lived here in Collinsport for years. I manage the family fish-packing plant and I wouldn't care to live anywhere else or move around as Barnabas does."

"It's a matter of taste," she said.

"What do you do back in London?" Roger Collins wanted to know.

"I was a photographer's model," she said.

"Doesn't surprise me," Roger said. "You're a very pretty girl. English type of beauty, of course. But I like the slim, pale look."

"Thank you," she said.

"And like all gentlemen, I prefer blondes," he said with a self-conscious laugh.

She was startled that he had undergone a complete change of manner. He actually seemed on the borderline of becoming amorous. She said, "I'm happy to meet other members of the Collins family. And you're being very kind to go to such trouble for me."

"Not at all," Roger protested. "Glad to be of some service. And don't think Barnabas is the only man in the Collins family with charm. Both he and Quentin are given too much credit for their personalities, if you ask me. There are young women who prefer the sounder qualities to mere charm."

"I'm sure of it," she said.

"That's where I shine, Miss Marriot," Roger assured her. "Keep that in mind. Don't lose your heart to Barnabas before you look over the other males available."

"I've not come here for any romantic reason," she told him.

"But romance might catch up with you," was Roger Collins' opinion. "Keep an open mind on the subject. And be sure and visit us at Collinwood. Here we are! This is the old house."

They halted and she strained to make out the lines of the red brick house which was partially veiled by the falling snow. It seemed smaller than the new Collinwood, and all its windows were shuttered.

"You'd not believe there was anyone in there," she said. "No lights are showing from the windows." Roger stood there bleakly gazing at the house with her bag still in his hand.

"Barnabas is in there just the same. He hardly ever opens the shutters. And his man Willie will be there if Barnabas should be out for one of his night walks."

"In a storm like this?" she wondered.

"Barnabas pays scant attention to the weather," Roger Collins told her. "I'll knock on the door and see who is at home." And he did. Then he added, "By the way, Barnabas and I get on each other's nerves. So if he's at home I'm going to allow you to go in on your own. Is that all right?"

The idea was attractive to her. She'd worried about how she was going to greet Barnabas without giving away the fact that she didn't know him. But with Roger away from the scene there would be no problems.

She said, "I don't mind. I think I prefer greeting him alone."

"Great," Roger said.

The door opened a crack and a young man stared out at them rather sullenly. "What do you want?"

Roger said, "I have a friend of Barnabas here. Would you show her in to my cousin?"

"All right," the young man said and swung the door open to reveal a dark hallway.

Roger Collins thrust her bag in the young man's hands. "This is Miss Marriot's bag," he said. "I'll let you take care of it, Willie."

She turned to Roger and said, "Thank you again."

He had doffed his fur cap and was standing on the steps in the falling snow. "My great pleasure," he said with a rare smile. "I shall anticipate our next meeting." With a bow, he put on his hat, and vanished into the stormy darkness.

The young man known as Willie told her, "You come along with me, miss." And he closed the door and led her down a hallway to double doors on the right. "Wait in here," he said.

She entered the living room of the old house which also had a blazing log fire in the marble fireplace. The room was smaller than the living room at Collinwood but just as richly furnished. She had the impression that the Collins family must be an old and wealthy one.

And where was she going to fit in all this? She had traveled half a world to arrive in this elegant, old-fashioned living room, to meet this man whom she'd never seen before. All on the slim hope that he might be able to help her. What if it should all turn out to be a macabre joke on Nurse Chisholm's part? She didn't dare think of the possibility. It would be too cruel!

The truth was that the long ordeal of the journey had exhausted her stock of energy as well as her stock of money. She was now in a desperate state. And there was the curse of her being a vampire. Tonight she'd been forced to take a terrible risk which could have landed her in prison to get enough blood from that waitress to survive. Another night would soon come and she would again know that terrifying need for human blood! She could only pray that before anything of that sort happened, this stranger she'd traveled so far to consult would be able to help her.

From all that she'd heard, he must be a good and generous man, with considerable charm. The portrait had given her some impression of what he might look like. She heard a board creak behind her and wheeled around with some alarm showing on her lovely face.

"Good evening, Miss Marriot," the man standing in the doorway said. He had the same gaunt, handsome face as the one she'd seen in the portrait. His brown hair was long and a lock strayed across his high forehead. But his eyes, under shaggy brows, were his chief features. Those deep-set, burning, kindly eyes.

She faltered. "You know my name."

He smiled somberly. "Don't be frightened by what appears to be mind reading," he said. "Your name was clearly marked on the tag attached to your bag—Adele Marriot of London, England. I don't believe I've ever had the pleasure of meeting you before."

Adele felt less afraid. "No," she said, "we've never met."

"And yet you've come here to see me," he said. "And you appear familiar with my name."

"I am," she said. "It was given to me by someone."

He looked interested. "Indeed?"

"Someone who knew that I needed help. And who felt that you might be able to supply it," she said.

"I see." His burning eyes seemed to be penetrating her mind. "Won't you sit down?"

"Thank you," she said. And she seated herself on the straight-back chair nearest to her.

"How did you know where to find me?"

"I went to your flat in London," she said. "Your housekeeper told me where you had gone."

He nodded. "I see. And why have you sought me out this way?"

"It's rather a long story," she said unhappily.

"Tell it to me in your own way," he said. And he moved across to stand by the fireplace. He was wearing a brown tweed suit.

She hesitated, then said, "You may have seen my photograph in some of the London magazines. I've been a fashion model for quite a while."

"You do seem somewhat familiar," Barnabas agreed.

"I've always had a weight problem," she went on in a strained voice. "Some weeks ago I went to Switzerland for a holiday. And while I was there I met a doctor who owned a clinic which he claimed was devoted to operating on overweight people and correcting a glandular condition. He offered to give me the operation free, and like a fool I accepted." Her words trailed off on a bitter note.

Suddenly Barnabas Collins was frowning. And in an angry voice he said, "You're speaking of Doctor Stefan Spivak, aren't you?"

Startled, she said, "Yes. How did you know?"

"I'm familiar with the story and his practices," Barnabas said. "How could you be so mad as to be taken in by his offer?"

She shook her head despairingly. "I don't know! I think he's a hypnotist. I seemed to fall under his spell."

"He may have hypnotic powers," Barnabas Collins said grimly. "It would explain a lot. You know the sort of monster he is?"

"I do now. When I discovered what had happened to me, I got your name from an English nurse working for him. Someone who couldn't return to England because she is wanted by the police."

"A murderess by the name of Beryl Chisholm," Barnabas said in a disgusted voice. "One of Spivak's stable of criminals."

Adele nodded. "So now you know," she said in a dull voice. "When I came off his operating table, he had made me one of the living dead. That's why I'm here to ask your help."

He studied her for a moment in silence. "My help?"

"I have been told that you've helped others in my plight," she said, her eyes fixed on him pleadingly.

"I have had the sad experience of meeting some of Spivak's victims," Barnabas Collins said. "He's not even a real doctor, you know. He picked up what he knows about surgery as an orderly in the German medical corps in the Second World War."

"He's very clever. I never guessed."

"Few people do. That's why he finds so many easy victims. He talks like a great specialist."

"I know."

The gaunt, handsome face was grim. "And he is clever with a scalpel. He has hit on a way of making a fortune. He must be a millionaire many times over. He made you a vampire but at the same time he cured someone else. And that someone else paid him a fortune for the cure."

"That is what Lisa must have meant by opposites," she exclaimed.

"Lisa?"

"A woman who was at the hospital when I was there," she said. "I'm sure she was a vampire there to be cured. She asked me if I had an opposite and laughed at me when I didn't understand. She told me I'd find out soon enough."

"As you did."

"Yes. Some of the people in the clinic seemed mad. They dressed and acted like people from another age. People from a past century."

Barnabas shook his head. "You haven't a clear conception of what is going on in that clinic yet. Those people you believed mad are from another century. Vampires have no life span, they roam as the living dead for years. Some of those people you saw might be more than one or two hundred years old, lost souls living in the shadows, and they had come to Spivak for a cure, willing to pay him anything."

"So he takes from the normal to salvage the cursed," she said.

"Not from any kindness," Barnabas assured her. "It is all evil and profit with him. He is a monster. And that castle is a place of lost souls."

She shuddered. "Terrible things happen there."

"It has been going on too long," Barnabas said.

"You've known about it for some time?"

"Yes," he nodded. "And if you wonder why I haven't done anything to halt his activities, I can only reply that I haven't been able to. He has been careful to masquerade his operation there as a normal one. So the authorities haven't been able to prove anything against him."

"They may soon," she said. "The innkeeper in the nearby village told me that he has made complaints. And now the police and health people are watching the clinic more closely."

"Let us hope they find him out," Barnabas said.

"I'll do anything I can to stop his awful game," she said.

"We'll think about that," Barnabas said. "I wonder that you managed to get all this way in your present state without anyone to help you."

She smiled up at him ruefully. "I almost didn't get here."

"You could only travel at night. You needed blood regularly."

"Yes," she agreed. "Earlier tonight I was desperate. I sent for room service. And when the maid brought me the tray I attacked her. I took an awful chance. But I had no choice."

"I understand," he said. "When you came here you went to the new Collinwood first?"

"Yes. Your cousins were kind to me. I pretended that I already knew you. I didn't dare do otherwise."

"What did you tell them about yourself?" he asked.

"Nothing. Except that I came from London and I was a model."

"Wise."

"They never would have understood if I'd told them the truth about myself," she said. "The truth of why I've come to you."

"That's certainly true," Barnabas said dryly.

"I asked your cousin Roger to bring me here without delay," she said.

"And he did?"

"Yes."

Barnabas smiled thinly. "It can only have been because of your lovely face. Roger doesn't like me. He never comes here. But he has an eye for a pretty girl."

"I gathered that."

Barnabas moved across the dimly lighted room before her and then sat heavily in a chair that was almost opposite her. He stared at her for a long moment again. "You have come so far, I must try to help you," he said at last.

"I'll be grateful to you forever if you can save me," she said.

He raised a warning hand. "I made no promises. I said I would try."

"That's enough."

His handsome face was expressionless as he said, "I'll have to be a bit personal in my questioning. I hope you won't mind. Are you married or engaged to anyone?"

"I was engaged," she said. "When I found out what had happened to me, I couldn't bear to have him know. So I sent him away."

"That's a familiar story," Barnabas said sadly.

"I have no parents living and no near relatives. So I'm alone and free in the world as far as ties are concerned."

Barnabas said, "I needed to know that. If I'm to help you, there are bound to be certain risks which anyone near and dear to you might not want you to accept."

"I'll face any risk to be cured," she said.

"I realize that," Barnabas said quietly.

"Do you have any plan for helping me?"

"There is a clinic not too far from here. It is not the type run by Spivak but a real hospital dedicated to the honest cure of its patients. I think its head, Doctor Julia Hoffman, may be interested in your case."

She leaned forward in her chair. "What are the chances of a cure?"

"Only fair," Barnabas said. "Those under the spell of a vicious curse are the worst off. You were actually made a vampire through surgery. She may be able to treat your case."

"I don't want to go on living if she can't," Adele cried.

Barnabas rose with a grim smile on his handsome face. "I'm sorry. You have no choice about that. As one of the living dead you'll walk the night shadows until you're somehow released."

"No!" She also rose to her feet.

"You will have to stay here with me if I'm to keep your secret from the others," Barnabas said.

"They mustn't find out."

"They needn't as long as you remain here," he said. "You will sleep through the days vampire fashion. And at night you will come to the kind of living you know now."

"I can't believe I'm a phantom!"

"But you are at the moment," he said. "You must be strong and face it. It is one of the things any of the living dead have to do. It marks the first step toward salvation."

"I'll do anything you say."

His eyes met hers solemnly. "There is the matter of blood. The blood you will need for survival."

Her eyes opened wide in alarm. "How can I find it here? The place is so isolated. There are no people but your family. I can't feast on their throats."

"We must find a means," Barnabas said in his quiet, forceful way. "There is the village not so distant when the weather is fine. I make certain forays there at suitable intervals."

"You?" Her voice fell to a whisper.

He nodded. "Yes. I thought you understood that. Like yourself I'm one of the living dead. Only I'm much worse off than you. I've lived under the shadow of a curse for over a hundred years. Not even Julia Hoffman has been able to help me in her clinic. And I refused your Doctor Spivak's way long ago when he made me an offer."

CHAPTER 6

This revelation on the part of the gaunt, handsome Barnabas shocked her. Up until this moment she had believed that he was merely a friend to the living dead and not one of them himself. But as she thought back, it became clear that he was indeed a vampire. The easy way in which his housekeeper in the London flat had accepted her should have made her suspicious; and then the fact that he lived alone in this old house rather than as a guest at the new Collinwood, and that he was a confirmed night person. It was all part of a pattern.

"So you are actually one of the living dead," she said, awed.

"Yes," he said in his pleasant voice with it's hint of a British accent. "Didn't you understand that?"

"No. I thought you were someone sympathetic to the plight of those like me."

"I am both sympathetic and one of you," Barnabas Collins assured her. "And as I have pointed out, there are various types of vampires, and only some of them are evil."

She gave him a meaningful look. "But we all require our nightly supply of blood which surely makes us potential killers."

"Only if we gorge ourselves until we have the last drop of blood in anyone's body. Then that person dies and automatically becomes one of the living dead. Just the wicked and demented among us take blood from ordinary humans to the point where death is caused."

Adele listened with disbelief. "You talk as if our numbers were legion."

"There are many more of us than most people will realize or admit," the handsome man said.

"What about your cousins, Elizabeth and Roger? Do they know?"

"They must but they pretend not to. Several times there have been complaints from the villagers about me. This occurs when some evil vampire comes here and does something for which I am blamed. I've had a number of such experiences," he told her with a bitter smile. "It appears there is something about Collinsport which attracts those living in the halfway world between life and death."

"Is that why Roger claims not to like you—because he thinks you are a vampire?"

"Yes. He's very touchy about the family reputation."

"I can tell that he's a proud, difficult man," she agreed. Barnabas moved over by the fireplace and put another birch log on the dying fire.

"Yes," he said, "I think we can assume that both Elizabeth and Roger are convinced that I'm one of the living dead. But they think it better not to make any reference to it."

"I'm sure it is," she said.

"They would be doubly upset if they were to discover what you are."

She stared at the handsome man standing before the fireplace. "When and where did it happen to you?"

"Here in Collinsport," he said sadly. "Nearly two centuries ago."

She gasped. "Almost two hundred years ago!"

"Yes."

"I can't believe it!"

There was an expression of amused irony on his gaunt face. "It is hard for me to realize at times. But I have wandered the earth all those years."

"So that it has to be your portrait in the foyer of Collinwood, not that of any ancestor."

"You are right."

"But you haven't told me how it happened."

"I met and married a beauty from the island of Martinique. Angelique and I were married in that island of romance and voodoo and came here to this house to live. I did not guess then that she was a practitioner of witchcraft and from the beginning had cast a spell on me."

"When did you first learn the truth?" Adele asked.

"Trouble developed soon enough," Barnabas said. "Joshua Collins, my father, brought the Countess DuPray and her lovely raven-haired daughter, Josette, here with him on his return from a visit to Paris. Not knowing of my marriage, he hoped that I might fall in love with Josette and she would make a fine wife for me.

Angelique was highly jealous and we quarreled. It was then she taunted me with the truth about her powers as a sorceress."

"And what was your reaction?"

Barnabas sighed. "I don't think I really believed her. Angelique left me and went back to her island in the West Indies. Josette remained in Collinsport and we were together a great deal. Soon I knew I was in love with her. Then I was stricken with a plague-like disease. The work of Angelique. I slipped into a kind of coma, and while I was in this helpless state a bat flew into my room and bit me on the throat. My father was the only one who happened to see this. He kept it a secret, suspecting that through the evil magic of Angelique I had been condemned to the vampire curse. That was the beginning of it. I was buried and a night later rose from my grave lusting for blood for the first time."

"How awful!"

"It was a horror I could not bear at the start," Barnabas admitted. "Since then I have learned to accept my fate. Several times I have been cured for short intervals. But the cure has never lasted. All the people I knew and loved at the beginning of my life are dust and crumbled bones now. So I have tamed my affections to those innocents condemned to a fate like my own. People like yourself."

"For which I can be grateful."

"Tomorrow night I shall drive you to Doctor Julia Hoffman's," he promised, "and we shall have her verdict as to whether you may be cured."

"What is this Doctor Hoffman like?"

"An unusual woman who has both intelligence and good looks. Were things different, I could easily have fallen in love with her. There was a brief romance between us once when I felt I might be permanently cured. When I reverted to the vampire state I told her there was no future for us. And that is how it stands now."

Adele gave him a searching look. "Was that fair? If she loves you she may not mind what you are."

His deep-set eyes met hers. "If I remember your story correctly, you sent your fiance away. Why expect me to feel differently?"

"I'm sorry," she said. "Of course you did the right thing. What about this youth who works for you?"

"Willie? He is a normal human being. I employ him because he is loyal and trustworthy. You may rely on him as I do."

"In our position you need someone who knows to assist," she said.

"I found that out long ago," Barnabas said. "Let me show you through the house and find you a room. Then you must rest."

"I'm weary," she admitted. "But I'm afraid to be alone when I'm awake. The thought of what has happened to me brings me to the edge of madness."

"You mustn't think about it," he told her.

"I find it impossible not to."

"As time passes you will gradually adjust," Barnabas Collins said. "The house here has been restored and is comfortable. But we do not have any electricity. Personally, I prefer candlelight." He picked up a candelabrum from the table.

"I adore it," she said. "Most women do, since it is soft and flattering to them."

Barnabas smiled. "I think it also gives rooms an enchanted air. We'll begin on this floor and then I'll move on to the others."

The tour of the ancient mansion proved fascinating. All the rooms were as well furnished as the living room. Finally he paused at a door which led to a dark stairway going down to the cellar.

His gaunt, manly face was solemn. "Would you care to see where I sleep?"

She hesitated. "Yes. Perhaps I should."

"Watch your step on the stairs," he warned her, holding the candelabrum high. "They are very steep."

She made her way down with Barnabas only a step behind her. Then he took the lead with the flickering candles held aloft as he marched along the darkness of the huge cellar. They came to a door in the far end and he opened it and went inside.

There was a wry expression on his face as he said, "Not a rich or very soft bed, but one I have become accustomed to."

She turned, and an expression of fear crossed her face as she found herself looking at a gray casket on a stand in the corner of the room. "You sleep in that?" she asked in awe.

"Always," he said. "When I travel it goes along with me. Willie looks after it if I happen to be inside it during the daylight hours. That is why he is invaluable to me."

She turned her back to the casket. "Forgive me for being shocked," she said. "I haven't any right. I'm as much a living corpse as you. But the sight of the coffin still revolts me."

"Then we won't remain here," Barnabas said. "I'll take you upstairs to your room."

Her room was on the second floor, and with the windows fully shuttered no trace of daylight would seep in while she was asleep. It was a small room and the four-poster bed was not an elaborate one, but she was sure she would be comfortable in it.

He placed the candelabrum on the dresser. With a sad smile, he said, "There is no mirror in this room. But since you have no reflection, you will not need one."

She nodded. "When I first discovered that, it was a nasty shock."

Barnabas stood in the doorway, a noble figure in the candlelight. "I hope you will be comfortable," he said. "If there is anything else you wish, Willie will get it. We'll meet tomorrow evening at dusk. During these winter months it comes shortly after five. So we'll have plenty of time to make the trip to Doctor Hoffman's place."

"What will you tell your cousins about my being here?"

"I've been considering that," he said. "I think I'll tell them we met at one of the photographer's studios where you modeled. And that you're over here to talk to me about doing a photography book on the theater. They know I'm interested in the theater and its people."

She smiled wanly. "Just so long as we have the same story. I think Roger will be asking me a lot of questions."

"Depend on it. He is sharp and suspicious. Especially where I'm concerned," Barnabas said. "Goodnight, Adele. I want you to try and forget the horror you've been through and relax in the knowledge you have a friend in me."

She looked up into his handsome face. "Thank you, Barnabas Collins."

"Meeting you has given me extreme pleasure," he said with a smile. And he went out, closing the door after him.

She stood there motionless for a moment. It was like a strange dream. She couldn't believe that she had crossed the ocean and was in a strange land. But here she was, the guest of Barnabas Collins. Until she'd reached this old house, Barnabas Collins had been only a name to her, but now she had met him and saw him as someone who might change her entire life and save her.

The shutters on the windows cut her off completely from outside. She had no idea whether the storm had ended or gotten worse. Did it really matter? She had a sanctuary and the protection of someone she greatly admired. For there was no doubt the impact of the handsome man's personality had registered strongly with her.

She paced nervously, unable to stretch out on the bed and relax. The many things Barnabas had told her raced through her mind. He was a vampire also. And he had been cast into this dire state through witchcraft, which he claimed made a cure more difficult. She knew so little about it all. And she found it impossible to understand the time differences in this world of the living dead. Barnabas claimed he was almost two hundred years old, yet she saw him as her own contemporary.

Dr. Julia Hoffman offered hope for her just as the diabolical Dr. Stefan Spivak had condemned her to this existence of the half-dead. She shuddered as she thought of that gray old castle and its sinister people. What was happening there now? Were other innocents like herself being betrayed into allowing him to operate on them? The evil should be stopped.

Slowly a great sleepiness came to her. And she knew that dawn must be at hand. Already she was beginning to know the signs. She tried to picture Barnabas going downstairs and getting into that coffin to spend the day but found it too fantastic. With a yawn she stretched out on the bed and lay on her back with her hands folded neatly on her breast. Then she slept.

There was someone moving in the room and she opened her eyes. It was Willie, who had brought in another candelabrum with three freshly burning white candles. He put it on the dresser and glanced at her nervously.

She raised up on an elbow. "Has another dusk arrived?" she asked.

"Yes. Dusk settled a few minutes ago. That is why I brought you fresh candles," he said.

"Thank you. Is your master up?"

Willie nodded. "Yes. He has just left to go over to Collinwood and borrow the car."

"I see. Is the storm over?"

"It ended this morning. The roads are all plowed but there was a heavy fall of snow," Willie said.

"Thank you, Willie," she said. "I'll be downstairs shortly."

"Yes, Miss," the youth said in a low voice and left the room.

Adele was impressed by the quiet competence of Willie. And Barnabas had said he was loyal. She wondered how Barnabas would make out at Collinwood – what questions would his cousins ask about her? She would be interested in hearing these things when he returned. Now she freshened up. She still had pride in her appearance though she could not benefit from the guidance of a mirror in making up.

By the time she made her way downstairs, the thing which she had feared was beginning to nag her. The thirst for blood! It came upon her each night shortly after she rose from her vampire sleep. And it was like a mad compulsion! Much stronger than hunger or thirst for ordinary food or drink. It made her tremble.

She was standing in the living room with her back to the door and her hands clasped before her in an effort to control herself when she heard someone in the hallway. She turned, her face distorted by her need, and looked at Barnabas with shame in her lovely eyes.

Barnabas, in a coat with a cape, came quickly to her. "I know," he said.

"It's dreadful!" She closed her eyes in an effort to gain control of herself.

He grasped her by the arms. "Try not to think about it."

"I can't! It's too strong to fight!"

"You can do better than that," Barnabas told her. "Come, we'll get into the car at once. If I drive quickly we can reach Doctor Hoffman's in a couple of hours."

She gasped, "I can't stand it that long."

"You must. Keep in mind Julia has blood stocked there. The moment we arrive she'll have a transfusion ready for you. I'll see that Willie phones ahead to arrange it."

She was in an abject state now. "I'll try to manage," she said in a hoarse whisper. "But don't leave me! Not for a moment! I can't answer for myself if you do."

His grip on her arms was firm. "Don't worry about that. I mean to stay with you." Then he called out for Willie. Almost at once the young man came into the room wearing a frightened look. He told him, "Phone Doctor Hoffman and tell her I'm on my way there with a patient, that she'll need a blood transfusion the moment we arrive. Julia will understand."

"Yes, sir," Willie said.

Barnabas began leading Adele out of the room. "You'll be better in the car," he promised. "This thirst hits you in waves. In a few minutes this one will subside, and it may be twenty minutes or more before you're subjected to it again."

It turned out that he was right. They were in the car and driving past Collinwood when she realized the compulsion for blood was easing. She sank back against the seat with a sigh. It was a small victory, but with the aid of the handsome man behind the wheel she'd won it.

He glanced at her as they drove along the road lined with banks of fresh snow. "You're better?"

Weakly, she said, "Yes."

"I knew you would be," he said. "Try not to think about it."

She gave him a pathetic look. "Will I go on having to endure these spells? I'm like a drug addict. I'm willing to do anything! I'd commit any crime to get blood!"

His noble profile was grim as he kept his eyes on the road ahead. "You don't have to tell me about it."

"You've gone on all through the years," she said in awe. "I don't know why you're not mad."

"Madness would be the coward's way out," he said. He turned on the headlights as it was getting dark.

She glanced back at Collinwood House, which they had just driven by. "Did they ask you about me?"

"Yes."

"What did they say?"

"Both Elizabeth and Roger were impressed by you. They felt you were most attractive."

"If they only knew," she sighed.

"You are attractive no matter what," Barnabas said.

"Did they want to know what I was doing at Collinwood?"

"Of course."

"What did you tell them?"

"What we agreed. You're working with a photographer in England and you've come here to see if I'll collaborate on the text of a book about theater. You see, I'm supposed to spend my solitary daytimes working on a family history. So I have the reputation of being a writer."

"It fits in nicely," she said.

He gave her an amused glance. "Roger is especially curious about you. I would say you've made a conquest there."

"I didn't try to."

"I told you he has an eye for a pretty girl," Barnabas reminded her. "And he now thinks you should be staying with him and Elizabeth rather than with me."

She smiled wanly. "I'm afraid he would quickly be disillusioned about me."

"We mustn't have that," Barnabas said. "It's important to have Roger on our side. Otherwise he might have one of his angry fits and ask us both to leave. He's done that to me before."

She stared at the man at the wheel. "You want me to encourage him?"

"Just mildly," Barnabas said.

"I'll try," she said. "I'll find it difficult."

"I don't think so," Barnabas told her. "I borrowed the car with the excuse that you've not been feeling well since you left London and I was of the opinion Doctor Hoffman should give you a check-up."

"That was no lie. I haven't been feeling well."

"I knew we'd be going up to Julia's clinic again, so I wanted to lay the foundation for an excuse for other times. We'll say she's concerned that your lungs aren't all they should be or something like that. I have my station wagon in the garage in Collinsport and it won't be available for a week or so. I have to borrow this car from them in the meantime."

"I'm a terrible lot of trouble," she said. "I have no right to impose myself on you this way."

"You have every right."

"You can't be grateful to that Nurse Chisholm for her giving me your name," she said.

"Beryl Chisholm is an evil woman," Barnabas said quietly. "But every so often she tries to make up for her wicked life by doing someone a good turn. That's why she's sent occasional unfortunates from the clinic to me."

"How does she happen to know about you?"

"A long story," Barnabas said. "When Doctor Spivak approached me about having an operation to be cured, he told me about Beryl. I remembered when she'd fled England after having murdered her husband. Later when I went to the clinic we talked. And when I discovered that my being cured meant condemning another person to being a vampire, I refused Spivak's offer. It was then we quarreled and I left. But not before I told Beryl how I felt and that when the opportunity presented itself I would try to break up Spivak's greedy scheme."

"So far you haven't," she said.

"Not so far," he admitted. "But I still have that goal in mind."

"I hope you're successful."

They reached the main highway, where there was more traffic even on this winter evening. Barnabas concentrated on his driving as she sat back in silence for a little. The torturing thirst for blood was returning and she needed all her concentration to keep it in control. Casual conversation was beyond her at this time. Barnabas apparently understood, for he made no attempt to talk.

After what seemed an endless drive they turned off the main

highway to a road flanked with tall evergreens whose branches were mantled with snow. The surface of this road had not been cleared as well as the main highway and so was more bumpy.

They came to a low brick fence with an entrance marked by two wrought-iron lamps mounted on black posts. The frosted faces of the lamps bore the lettering Hoffman Clinic. The driveway to the entrance was as wide as the road and the brick building was several stories high. Lights showed at its windows.

Barnabas glanced at her as he brought the car to a halt. "We've made it," he said.

She nodded weakly. "Yes."

He got out and opened the car door for her and helped her up the granite steps to the entrance of the clinic. Through the glass panels of the doors she could see the lobby and a dark-haired woman in a green smock talking to a white-uniformed nurse. The woman had an attractive, intelligent face and Adele at once decided that she must be Dr. Julia Hoffman.

This was confirmed when Barnabas took Adele inside. He greeted the woman with a tense, "Are you all ready for us, Julia?"

The dark woman nodded. "I've been waiting." She gave Adele a sympathetic smile. "Come along with me, Miss Marriot."

Adele went with her in a blurred state of mind. She didn't take any stock of her surroundings until about ten minutes later after the transfusion began to take effect. Then the hospital room began to come into focus and she took note of its white walls and neat equipment. She was stretched out on a bed with the transfusion apparatus set up beside her. As the blood dripped into her arm, Dr. Julia Hoffman stood on the other side of the bed studying her.

Dr. Hoffman said, "I can see that you are coming around."

"Thank you, yes."

"I'm sorry you had such an ordeal," the doctor said with a sigh. "I know what such torment can mean."

Adele's eyes widened with surprise. "Were you ever—?" She let the question trail off.

Julia Hoffman understood her. "No. I have never been one of the living dead. But I have had many patients who've been in this condition, so I have intimate knowledge of the sufferings involved."

"Barnabas says you may be able to cure me."

"I can't tell you much about that for the moment," she said frankly. "I plan to spend most of this night on tests. Only then will I be able to make any prediction about your case."

Fear showed in Adele's eyes. "We must be back at Collinwood before dawn," she said.

"I understand that," Julia Hoffman said patiently. "When I was treating Barnabas he would remain here until the early morning. But he always gave himself time to make the drive back before dawn."

"I don't like to ask you to work all night with me," Adele said. "It isn't fair to you."

Dr. Julia Hoffman said, "I consider it an opportunity. I'm still in the experimental stage in this work. Every new patient offers me additional knowledge."

"You know how I came to be like this?"

"Barnabas told me. You are one of Doctor Stefan Spivak's victims. And I have seen quite a few of them. He is a monster. His clinic should be closed and he should be jailed. I think it is only a question of time until that happens."

"I don't know what I would have done except for Barnabas," she told the older woman.

Dr. Hoffman smiled sadly. "You don't have to laud Barnabas to me. I'm a warm admirer of his."

"And he is very fond of you," Adele said.

The woman doctor glanced at the transfusion bottle to see how much blood was left in it. It was almost empty. She moved around to the other side of the bed, ready to disconnect it, and at the same time told Adele, "He has suffered from the same fate as yourself for a very long time. Once he returned to normal for several months. I was sure he was cured. But the curse proved too strong. He was stricken again."

"Barnabas told me that all cases are not the same. He said I might be easier to cure."

"I'm hoping so," Dr. Hoffman said. "We'll begin the tests now and then we'll see."

Adele remained on the bed as the doctor took blood specimens from her and gave her injections of seven or eight different drugs. There were periods of waiting, and then the doctor took her temperature reading, her pulse and checked her eyes with a strong light. These and other tests were repeated again and again.

Adele felt strange because of the drugs. She wondered what they were. At last Dr. Julia Hoffman told her there was no need to remain on the bed any longer. She had finished with the tests. They went out of the hospital room to Dr. Hoffman's large private office, where they found Barnabas seated in an easy chair reading a medical volume.

He rose at once and put the book aside. His gaunt, handsome face showed tension as he asked, "What is the word on the tests?"

Dr. Hoffman hesitated. "I dislike making a final diagnosis until I have gone over the case with my colleague, Professor Stokes, and he is away at the moment. But I have discovered the usual pituitary transplant and resultant damage. I think there is only one real hope of curing Miss Marriot and that is a slim one."

CHAPTER 7

A dele listened to the doctor's words and felt a thrill of hope.
Even a slim chance was better than none. It meant there was a
possibility that she might once again become a normal human being.
She asked Julia Hoffman, "Would you please explain?"

Barnabas said, "Yes, Julia, I'm anxious to know the facts."

Julia Hoffman placed the sheaf of report sheets she'd been
holding on her desk before she replied. "The operation which Doctor
Spivak performs is not always one hundred percent successful.
As you know, in addition to the actual transfer of tissue involved
between the normal person and the vampire victim, there is another
factor. I might best describe it as a sort of physical extrasensory
perception, an ESP of the tissues. In some cases the benefits of this
wear off. And as a result the vampire gradually returns to being a
vampire and the donor of the tissue just as surely becomes a normal
person again."

Adele said, "You mean the operation may lose its value and I
will slowly lose my vampire tendencies?"

"Yes," Julia Hoffman said. "But that is, as I have pointed out,
a very slim chance."

Barnabas said, "That would depend on luck alone. Is there
anything positive we can do to help Adele?"

The woman doctor gave him a thoughtful look. "There is one

thing. If she knows who the vampire was who received her tissue, she could free herself of the curse by destroying her."

"I think I know who received my tissue," Adele said. "It was someone I knew as Lisa but whom the nurse at the clinic called the Countess Dario."

"The Countess Dario is a famous Italian beauty," Barnabas said at once. "She's internationally known as a society leader. And I have heard whispers that she is one of the living dead."

"I doubt if she is any longer," Adele said bitterly. "I talked to her at the clinic and she was awaiting an operation. Later, when I was taken into the operating room, I'm certain I saw her on the table beside me."

Barnabas looked excited by this information. He glanced at Dr. Hoffman. "What do you say to that, Julia?"

The attractive woman doctor turned to Adele. "Were you drugged when you went into the operating room?"

The question came as a surprise, for she knew that she had been given pre-medication. "Yes," she said.

"I thought so," Julia Hoffman said. "And I'm afraid that makes it doubtful if your impressions in that room are apt to be of any value."

Her hopes sagged. "You think I might have imagined seeing her there?"

"It could have been a drug fantasy," the woman doctor agreed. "You had seen her before and perhaps expected to see her there. And your drugged mind played a trick on you."

Adele sighed. "It could be. But I was certain I saw her there with a white sheet draped over her."

Barnabas spoke up, "You very well might have seen her. But Julia is merely warning you that you can't be absolutely sure. I'd say it's a good bet it was the Countess Dario who gained by your operation."

Dr. Hoffman said, "There is only one way to prove it. Seek out the woman and destroy her. If you at once regain normalcy you will know you were right. If there is no change, then you can be certain that you were wrong, that you didn't see her in the operating room."

"How could I hope to find her?" Adele asked in despair.

Barnabas said, "She usually spends the winters in Rome. I can make some inquiries. If she is living a normal life we'll know she's had Spivak's operation. But that still wouldn't prove that you were her opposite for the surgery. We'd have to find that out later."

Dr. Hoffman said, "Perhaps it's too early to worry about such things. First I want to go over all the tests I made with Professor Stokes. I suggest that you return here in a week, Adele."

"You won't know any sooner than that?" she asked anxiously.
The woman doctor shook her head. "I'm afraid not."

"I'll bring her back next week," Barnabas promised. "I'll
have Willie phone you, and you can let him know which is the best
evening."

"Of course," Julia Hoffman said.

Adele turned to him with troubled eyes. "What will happen
to me in the meantime?"

Barnabas spoke to the woman doctor. "What Adele is
concerned about is her nightly need for blood. She is a stranger at
Collinwood and somewhat confined by this winter weather."

The woman doctor turned to her. "I have a serum that will
take care of your problem. I have used it to help Barnabas in the past
but ran out of supplies for a while. Now I have it in quantity again.
I'll give you enough to last both of you until you return here next
week. It will supply your needs for blood until then."

Barnabas's handsome face brightened. "That is good news,
Julia." And to Adele he explained, "It's the next best thing to being
normal again. We still won't be able to function in the daytime. But
we can each take an injection of the serum when we awake at dusk
and as a result feel no desire for fresh blood."

Adele told the doctor, "That will make all the difference."

"I wish I could offer you full recovery," the older woman
said.

Barnabas smiled at Adele. "So you see things are not so bad
after all. I'm going to warm the car up for the drive back while you
get the serum from Julia. You can join me outside."

Julia Hoffman took Adele to a drug room down the corridor
from her office and selected the vials of serum and two hypodermic
kits. The attractive woman put them in a small carton and passed
them to her. She said, "This will be everything you'll need."

"I don't know how to thank you," Adele told her as she took
the carton.

Julia smiled sadly. "I'm always happy to be able to help
Barnabas or any of his friends."

"You're doing fine work here."

"I like to think so. Professor Stokes and I have dedicated
the clinic to mental and physical ailments bordering on
metempsychosis. The living dead present a great challenge for the
small skills we've acquired in this field."

"You've given me new hope," Adele said.

"I trust I won't have to disappoint you," Julia Hoffman
replied. "You know in a way I rather envy you."

Her eyebrows raised. "Envy me?"

"Yes. You share your condition with Barnabas. The shadow

under which you both are living binds you closely. As a normal human I can't hope to understand him in the same way."

"I hadn't thought of it like that."

"However horrible you may find this living death, at least you're having the adventure of experiencing it together."

A feeling of guilt ran through her. "I am selfish. All I've been thinking of is my own salvation. And Barnabas is worse off than I and he's turning all his efforts to helping me."

"That is typical of Barnabas," Julia Hoffman said with tenderness in her voice. "And while his Cousin Quentin has the same quality of kindness, he can be a puzzling person."

"I've not met Quentin."

"He has also been my patient," the woman doctor said. "He has another kind of problem. It would be better if he doesn't show up in Collinwood while you are attempting to straighten out your own situation."

If Adele had known the woman better, she would have asked her more about Quentin Collins. But at a first meeting she didn't like to show too much curiosity. And she also realized that time was getting short. They would barely be able to make the drive back to Collinwood before dawn. So she hastily thanked the doctor again, said goodbye and hurriedly left the clinic to join Barnabas in the waiting car.

"I'm sorry I was so long," she said, as she got in the front seat beside him.

"I've just got the engine running nicely," he said. "It's a cold night."

As they headed out toward the road, she asked, "Do you think we can reach the house before dawn?"

"We can if we don't have any delays."

"Let's trust we won't have any," she said.

His face was grim as he watched the road ahead. "I agree."

"What would happen if we were caught on the road and daylight came?" she inquired worriedly.

"We could either abandon the car and take refuge in some dark place until dusk showed again or remain in the car and be found as dead."

She was shocked. "They'd think we were really dead."

"As far as anyone who didn't know would be concerned, there would be two corpses in the front seat of this car," Barnabas said grimly. "Hard to say what they'd do with us. So our best chance would be to abandon the car and find a suitably isolated, deserted building and hide there."

"And if no one discovered us during our daytime coma we could emerge again at night and find our way back home."

"Exactly," he said. "It's a macabre situation to think about. Let's just hope nothing like that happens. You have the serum?"

"Yes. Dr. Hoffman is a wonderful woman."

He smiled sadly. "I agree."

In a quiet voice, Adele said, "You know she's still in love with you."

"Nonsense. That's all over."

"I don't agree."

He looked away from the road for a second. "Why do you say that?"

"It's pretty obvious to a woman," Adele said. "She's just as much in love with you as she ever was. Tonight she told me she envied me."

"Envied you?"

"Yes. Envied my being in the same vampire state as you. She felt it brings me closer to you than she could ever be."

He frowned as he kept busy at the wheel. Then he said, "I suppose in a way she's right. It's almost as if you and I belonged to the same family or to some special group."

"I hadn't thought about it that way," she said. "But it is true."

"It occurred to me last night when I first saw you at Collinwood," Barnabas said. "Don't think I'm not extremely sorry and concerned about you. But I also had some pleasure in your arrival. You are a beautiful girl as Roger points out. And at last there is someone with me at Collinwood who knows and understands me."

She was touched by his words. "Wandering in the night is a lonely business," she agreed. "Before I left the clinic I had taken to spending many of my nights roaming through a nearby cemetery. I had the feeling of being near my own kind."

"The true dead reach out to us," Barnabas said in a taut voice. "That is one of the great dangers. The desire to join them completely is sometimes so strong. And yet we can't do that even if we wanted to. At least not without help—someone to drive a stake of hawthorn through our hearts. Only that would bring an end to the loneliness and the wandering in the shadows."

"I don't want permanent death yet," she protested. "I'd still like to go back to a normal life for a while."

"So would I," Barnabas said. "Even though all the world I knew is dead. I would enjoy this new age we have today, imperfect as it may be."

"Surely Doctor Hoffman will find a way to save both of us," she said.

His eyes were on the road where the headlights exposed the treacherous surface of snow and ice. "I think from what she said she can at least cure you."

"There is one sure way. Find the Countess Dario and destroy her."

Barnabas frowned. "I don't think you should build on that. I agree with Julia. It's likely your seeing her on that operating table was pure drug fantasy. Your opposite in the surgery could have been anyone."

"I suppose so," she said, hope fading from her tone. They drove on but as they neared Collinsport she could see the first hint of dawn in the dark sky. She glanced at him nervously. "We're not going to have many minutes to spare."

Barnabas nodded grimly. "Touch and go."

"As long as we get to the old house Willie can take the car back to your cousins at Collinwood," she suggested. "No problem there."

They rounded a curve and all at once she saw a lot of blinking red lights ahead. There were also the beam of headlights twisted across the road. And as they drew closer she was able to see that a huge trailer-truck had jack-knifed on the ice and collided with a car. Other cars had come suddenly upon the accident scene and there had been a pile-up of two or three additional vehicles. It was a mess!

"Look out!" she screamed at Barnabas.

"I see it," he said as he jammed on the brakes.

Their car skidded ahead close to the glaring lights and wreckage of the accident scene before he could halt it. There was a state trooper's car with its revolving red roof light already on the scene. And now there was a trooper coming toward them with a large flashlight in his hand.

He bent down to look in the window at them, a solemn expression on his young face. "Don't drive any nearer folks. We've had a bad pile-up here."

Barnabas said, "Can we turn and go back to the next exit, we're in a hurry."

The trooper shook his head. "Too risky with the roads like this. You'll have to wait until we get cleared up a little."

"Will that take long?" Barnabas asked.

"Twenty minutes or so. There's a tow truck on the way," the trooper said.

"We're in a rush," Barnabas told him.

"Too much speed caused this accident," the trooper said grimly. "You'll be able to make up the time. It will be dawn in another three-quarters of an hour." And he moved off to return to the scene of the wreck.

Fear clutched at Adele's throat. "Three-quarters of an hour until dawn! What will we do?"

Barnabas had a haunted look on his face. "We'll have to be patient. If they take too long we'll simply pull the car over in the breakdown lane and make a run for it through the woods."

"Where?"

"We'll find some shelter," the man in the caped coat said grimly. "We're only a few miles from Collinsport."

She stared at the confusion of lights, the wrecked cars, and the men moving around aimlessly and shouting instructions, and felt they were surely trapped.

"They'll never get a passage cleared in time for us to reach Collinwood before dawn," she worried.

"We may," Barnabas said. "See, the tow truck has arrived. It's there now."

The tow truck had a powerful spotlight and she watched with bated breath while work began to move the big truck which had toppled on its side and was the chief block to the broad highway. Barnabas got out of the car and walked ahead to get a closer view. She could spot his caped figure outlined against the array of red, yellow and white car lights and the wreckage.

Time dragged on. She could hear the cries of the men as they called out directions. And she knew that they had already lost too much time. Soon it would be dawn and both she and Barnabas would freeze into the sleep of death until dusk came. As Barnabas had warned, anyone finding them in the car would presume them dead!

She clutched the carton with the serum to her and waited. Then she saw Barnabas slowly walking back. He got in the car, his face grim. "They'll be allowing us through in a moment," he said. "But we'll never make Collinwood now."

Panic showed on her pretty features. "What will we do?"

"The main thing is to get by this busy spot."

"And then?"

"Try to locate the nearest side road and some place to park the car and hide until dusk."

"Will we be able to find any such place in time?"

"We had better."

The trooper now was waving his flashlight for them to drive on. They drove ahead very slowly and saw that the tow truck had dragged the trailer truck far enough to one side to allow room for passing. The other cars were strewn around the road drunkenly, a confusion of twisted metal, broken glass and other wreckage. Then they passed the congestion and were able to pick up some speed. But now dawn was clearly streaking the sky ahead.

"There should be an exit in about a mile," Barnabas said.

"I'm beginning to feel drowsy already," she told him.

"I know the feeling," he said in a taut voice. "But we both must hold on until we get to safety."

"What about your cousins? When we don't get back?"

"They'll think we stayed overnight at the clinic."

"They won't be worried?"

"I hope not," he said. And he drove on.

At last they came to the exit. Barnabas drove off the expressway, losing the other cars that had been held up because of the wreck. They were on the outskirts of a town. They came to a division of the side roads and Barnabas took one that bore a sign advertising camps along the shore. It was obviously a summer vacation spot of some sort.

"This ought to be suitably remote," he said.

"My head is reeling," she told him weakly.

"The serum," he said. "Hide it in the glove compartment of the car. We can't keep it with us. Someone might come along and steal it. We can lock the car."

"I know," she said, fumbling with the latch of the glove compartment. She finally got it open and placed the precious carton inside. Then she closed the cover of the compartment. Her head was getting worse every moment. She knew she would soon sink into that dread state.

The road was lined with trees and not well plowed. But cars had been on it lately. In the glow of dawn you could see their wheel tracks. She glanced at Barnabas and saw that he looked more gaunt than ever. He was in as bad a condition as she was and still trying to drive on. It seemed he might collapse at any moment.

"Ahead on the right," he said weakly.

And a moment later he wheeled the car into a driveway a foot deep in snow. The car came to a jarring halt as she spied the summer cottage with its brown shingles and gray, boarded windows set in on the left. Barnabas shut off the car's engine and turned to her. His face was now a haggard caricature of the Barnabas she knew. His eyes seemed to have sunk deeper in his head and the lines at his mouth looked like great welts.

"We must lock the car and get inside somehow," he said in a hoarse voice.

"I know," she nodded. And she reached to open the car door on her side. She was shocked by her weakness. It was all she could do to shove the door ajar, and she stumbled out into the fairly deep snow. Meanwhile Barnabas had locked the door on his side and was sliding across the seat to join her.

He shut and locked the door on her side so that the serum and the car would be relatively safe. Then he took her by the arm and they began stumbling ahead through the snow to reach the deserted summer cottage.

"Get in somehow," he mumbled, his voice slurred.

They walked around to the rear of the cottage, and there in the back a vestibule window was without boards. Barnabas left her to find a birch log on a pile that had been cut for the fireplace and came back with a long sturdy one in his hand. He had a grim look on his face as he smashed the lower window pane with the log and then reached in and unlocked the sash so it could be raised.

She was leaning against the rear wall of the house, feeling that any moment she might lose consciousness. "What now?" she asked, and her voice sounded thin and far away.

The handsome man in the caped coat came to her and she was again alarmed by the change in him. He looked dreadfully old and weary. "I'll help you up to the sill. Then you should be able to get inside," he told her.

She was too far gone to make any protests as he led her to the window and then with a strength which she found surprising lifted her so she could grasp the sill and manage to scramble over it and drop to the rough board floor breathlessly. She dragged herself across the small vestibule to make room for Barnabas as he came through the window.

He joined her a moment later. Helping her to her feet, he guided her inside the house to the rooms darkened by the boarded windows. A tiny bit of light escaped around the edges of the boards and penetrated the rooms so they could see around them a little.

Barnabas hesitated in a shadowed doorway and told her, "We'll be all right here."

"You don't think anyone will come and find us?" she worried.

"I can't imagine anyone coming here unless they were hiding out like us," was his grim reply.

Her head was reeling. She felt she must find somewhere to rest. "I'm slipping away fast," she told him.

"I'm almost as weak," he said. "Here we are!" And he guided her into a room with twin beds. As they stepped into the room her legs buckled under her and she fell to her knees.

"I can't!" she moaned.

"It's all right," Barnabas said, lifting her up in his arms. But he was also weakened so that he wavered under the additional burden as he made his way to one of the beds with difficulty. Then he tenderly let her down. There was no pillow or any bedclothes. Just the plain mattress. But that didn't matter. He bent over her for a long moment, "You'll be safe now," he said. And for just a fleeting second he touched his lips to hers.

"Barnabas!" she murmured his name tenderly.

She was barely conscious of what was going on around her but she saw his shadowy form move to the bed opposite her and then collapse on it. He had exhausted his last ounce of strength.

Her eyes closed. She was quickly sinking into the sleep of death which would last until dusk. She could only pray that they would be safe here until then. She didn't dare think what would happen if anyone stumbled upon them. They would be regarded as repulsive dead creatures.

Suddenly she thought she heard someone in the shadowed bedroom. With a great effort she opened her eyes and stared up into the darkness. Her vision was blurred so that she could not see plainly at first. But as she focused her eyes she saw a man standing just inside the room gazing at them on the beds.

Fear shot through her and she tried to raise herself up and shout a warning cry to Barnabas. But she could neither move nor speak. She was caught in the icy, unrelenting grasp of death itself!

Through half-closed eyes she studied the intruder. And he seemed incredulous to the point of being a fantasy. He had a broad, solemn face and his skin was brown. His head, which was either completely bald or clean shaven, was of the same shade as his face. And in his ears were large golden earrings. He looked like a Buddhist priest she'd known in London.

She was still staring at this remarkable figure when her vision faded altogether. Then all feeling in her body ceased and she was lost to the world around her.

CHAPTER 8

Her waking was as gradual as had been her slipping off into that deep sleep. It was minutes before she was able to stir in the bed and raise herself on an elbow. She looked across at the other bed and saw that Barnabas was seated on it, gazing at her. He looked more like himself than the haggard creature she'd seen in those last minutes before she lost consciousness.

"We've survived," he said with a grim smile.

"Yes."

Barnabas got to his feet. "It was lucky we found this refuge. Now we can drive on to Collinwood."

As he spoke, remembrance came rushing back to her. She quickly rose and told him, "Someone was in here!"

"What?" He frowned.

Fear shadowed her pretty face. "I saw a man just before I lost consciousness. A strange-looking man!"

"Are you sure?"

"Yes." And she described him to Barnabas.

"Someone who looked like a Buddhist priest," Barnabas said doubtfully. "I can't imagine what he'd be doing here."

"Or why he didn't bother us."

"That's another interesting thing to speculate about," Barnabas said in a tense voice. "If this man really existed, where has he gone?"

"I don't know. But I did see him. He had golden circular earrings."

Barnabas eyed her grimly. "You remember all the details."

"He was so strange I couldn't forget. And he was watching us with a funny expression."

Barnabas said, "I don't know what to say about it. But we mustn't linger here. We should be getting on our way."

"I agree."

"We'll go straight to the old house. "We'll take time out to inject that serum and then drive back to Collinwood itself and make our explanations."

"Yes," she said, giving him a meaningful look. "I know I'll need the serum. The uneasiness is coming on me again."

Barnabas led the way out of the bedroom, and then as they reached the kitchen door he suddenly went rigid. For the man she had described was standing in the middle of the kitchen by a table with a lighted candle on it.

Barnabas was staring at the man with a strange expression on his handsome face. "It has to be you, Quentin," he said quietly.

The quivering flame of the candle glowed up on the man's face and he smiled. In a friendly voice he said, "That's most disappointing, Barnabas. I had counted on you not being able to recognize me."

"I mightn't have except for the circumstances," Barnabas said with a resigned look on his handsome face. But he was no longer so tense. He turned to her and said, "May I present Miss Adele Marriot. This is my wayward cousin, Quentin."

Quentin came over to her and took her hand. "Delighted to meet you, Adele. Barnabas always finds himself some charming girl companion. And you are up to his standards."

She blushed. "And I have heard about you."

"No good," Quentin said. "I'm positive of that."

"I've really only heard your name mentioned," she admitted.

"Then my reputation is secure for the moment," he said.

Barnabas gave him a questioning smile. "What does this shaven head mean? What has happened to your fine curly hair?"

"I have dispensed with it for a little," Quentin said with another of his ironical smiles. "I was forced to change my identity rather quickly to get away from an embarrassing situation. I hit upon this disguise. And it appealed to me so much I decided to make a brief visit to Collinsport and test it on Roger and Elizabeth. I had no idea the first of the family I'd encounter was to be you."

"How did you come to find us here?" Barnabas asked.

"I had your idea ahead of you. I've been using a summer

cottage across the road as my temporary headquarters. Like yourself I'm not bothered by the cold and I wanted a place to hide out if I needed to. Then you drove in here. I was watching from the window of the other cottage, thinking you were unwelcome intruders. Then I recognized you. I waited until you and Adele had gone inside and then I went in to double check."

"So I did see you in our room!" Adele said.

"Yes," Quentin agreed.

"At least you were here to keep an eye on us," Barnabas said.

"I felt I should," Quentin agreed mockingly. "After all, we are cousins and regarded by the rest of the family as the black sheep. So we must be loyal to one another."

Barnabas looked bleak. "This is going to be a rude surprise for Roger. Having us both here at once."

Quentin laughed. "It's possible he may not recognize me as easily as you did."

"True," Barnabas said. "Are you planning on a long stay?"

"Not really," Quentin said. "Since I'm never welcome at the main house, may I live with you in the old one? I seldom do, but now that you've seen through my disguise there's no point in my avoiding you."

Barnabas nodded. "You're welcome to a room. Do you want Roger and Elizabeth to know I have a guest? Shall I introduce you to them?"

Quentin shook his head. "Not yet. They might see through my disguise too. You've shaken my faith in it. Let me just wander around quietly for a little." He turned to her with a smile. "And get to know Adele better."

"Adele is not in the mood for flirtation," Barnabas warned his cousin. "You know she shares the curse of the living dead with me. Her purpose in being here is to seek help from Doctor Hoffman."

"You couldn't find a better doctor," Quentin told her.

"Were you ever treated by her?" she asked.

"Yes," he said. "Unfortunately, I proved too difficult a problem."

Barnabas said, "We have to get back to Collinwood as soon as possible. We've been away since early last evening and I have Roger's car."

"I have my own small car," Quentin said. "I'll follow a little later. If I came at the same time I'd attract too much attention." He glanced at Adele again. "How is it you are one of the night people?"

Barnabas spoke for her. "It's a tragic story. She submitted to an operation in Switzerland. Perhaps you've heard of Doctor Stefan Spivak and his evil clinic."

"Everyone in the fringe world has," he said. "Spivak should have been destroyed long ago. You have my sympathy, Adele."

"Thank you," she said quietly.

"With luck Julia may be able to cure her," Barnabas said. "But there is no guarantee."

"Life seldom offers us guarantees," the friendly Quentin said. "So we must learn to live with risk."

Barnabas turned to Adele with a smile. "Before Quentin becomes too philosophical, I think we should get underway."

They said goodbye to him and then got in the car as he stood watching after them, a strange figure in his heavy winter clothes with his bald head bare to the freezing night air. He waved at them as they backed out onto the narrow roadway. Their wheels spun a little but they managed to clear the snow.

At last they were on the way to Collinwood. It had been a strange and thrilling adventure, but so far they had come out of it relatively unscathed. She looked in the glove compartment and found the carton with the serum. She kept it on her lap.

As they reached the expressway again, she said, "Your cousin Quentin seems a nice person but very strange. Why that bizarre disguise?"

Barnabas sighed. "It's hard to say. Quentin has his own problems."

"So he said," Adele recalled. "What are they?"

"Like ourselves he suffers under a curse. He is one of the night people. But his curse is different from ours."

"In what way?"

"You've heard of people who at certain times take on the shape of wolves?"

Her eyes widened. "Werewolves? I always thought they were only found in horror movies. You can't be serious."

"Just as serious as when I say we are vampires," Barnabas told her. "Most people wouldn't believe our story. But we know what we are and why. So it is with Quentin."

"Is he at the mercy of the curse as we are?"

"There are times when he cannot protect himself from it," Barnabas said. "It happened more than once in Collinsport. So he became the subject of legends in the area. Most of the stories were exaggerated. But the family disowned and exiled him from the estate in a manner somewhat similar to the way they've treated me. Perhaps I'm even more welcome at Collinwood than Quentin because they find his behavior more terrifying."

"I thought him pleasant," she said.

"And so he is," Barnabas agreed. "But he is bitter as well. For which you can't blame him."

"You seem to be good friends."

"We have come to an understanding," Barnabas said.

"He was there to guard us last night. We owe him something for that."

"That's why I've offered him a room at the old house," Barnabas said. "I only hope he causes us no problems." They reached Collinwood and saw the lighted windows of the rambling mansion. And then they continued on to the old house. Inside, Willie had a pleasant log fire in the living room to greet them.

Barnabas smiled at her. "A little different from the cottage."

"Yes. It's fortunate the cold doesn't bother us."

"After we have the serum we'll take the car to Collinwood and spend a little time with Roger and Elizabeth. I imagine they've been wondering about us," Barnabas said.

It was a little before eight when they presented themselves at Collinwood. Elizabeth greeted them and a look of relief crossed her lovely face.

"We were worried about you," she told them. "What happened?"

"Doctor Hoffman wanted Adele to remain overnight for some tests," Barnabas said. "They took longer than we expected."

Elizabeth gave Adele a concerned look. "I hope you have no serious health problem?"

She said, "I'm sure Doctor Hoffman understands my trouble and will be able to do something about it."

"Though she has to return in a few days for another check-up," Barnabas added quickly.

"Well, you couldn't be in better hands," Elizabeth smiled. "Come into the living room and see Roger." When they went on to the elegantly furnished big room, Roger Collins was standing by the sideboard pouring himself a drink. He at once came to them.

"About time you were back," he said, giving Barnabas an annoyed look. "I understood you were returning last night."

Barnabas gave him the same story and said, "I felt sure you would endorse these precautions for the sake of Adele's health."

The stern Roger looked less annoyed. "By all means," he said. "But you might have let us know. Elizabeth and I have been concerned. In this winter weather there are all kinds of car accidents."

Elizabeth smiled at her brother. "I don't think we need make any more fuss about it. They are back safe and that's all that matters."

"It was kind of you to let us have the car," Adele said.

Roger was at her side and looking more friendly than usual. "You may have it any time."

Elizabeth and Barnabas moved on down by the fireplace, leaving Adele and Roger alone. Adele had an idea this was a deliberate move on Barnabas's part to give her a chance to exert her charm on Roger.

As they stood under the glow of an ornate crystal chandelier Roger asked, "Can I get you a drink of any kind?"

"Not just now," she said. "Thank you."

Roger glanced at the distant Barnabas and in a low voice confided to her, "You had better be on the alert with my cousin. Barnabas has a rather wicked reputation with females."

She registered mild surprise. "He's been very kind to me."

"Just watch him, that's all," Roger said darkly. "I'm not at all sure you should be staying at the old house with him. It could cause talk. You'd be better off to move over here with us."

"I can't see any need of it," she protested.

"Elizabeth would enjoy the company. We all would," Roger said earnestly. "I'd very much like to get to know you better."

"You're very kind," she said, pretending suitable gratitude.

"Life here is very lonely," Roger went on. "Especially in winter."

"I can understand that."

Roger gulped down the rest of his drink. Then, awkwardly, he said, "I'm a much more dependable person than Barnabas."

"I have no doubt that you are," she said, secretly amused. He was behaving exactly as Barnabas had predicted. "But you must admit that Barnabas has wonderful qualities of his own."

"A person of contradictions," Roger said stiffly, and it was evident this was as far as he was willing to go. "There has been a good deal of scandal attached to his name."

"I wouldn't have expected that."

"There are those in the village who are afraid of him," Roger went on. "I'm telling you this for your own good. Long ago his ancestor left here under a dark shadow, accused of being tainted with the vampire curse. Some people believe the curse has been handed down from generation to generation."

"How do you feel about it?" she asked.

Roger looked uncomfortable. "I think there may be some truth in it. A couple of times when Barnabas has been here living in the old house we've had attacks on several of the village girls. They've been left in a dazed state with weird marks on their throats. Typical of attacks by a vampire."

Adele looked toward the fireplace where Barnabas and Elizabeth were still talking and said, "I think those stories must have been made up. I can't see Barnabas as a vampire any more than I could see myself as one."

Roger looked shocked. "You mustn't say such things. You're one of the finest young women I've ever had the pleasure of meeting."

"You're too kind," she said.

"It's a fact. I'm considering marrying again. My son, David, should have a proper mother. Elizabeth and her daughter, Carolyn, are wonderful to him, but they can't take a mother's place. And if I were to select an ideal wife I'm sure it would be someone like yourself."

She smiled. "I'm afraid you're idealizing me without really knowing the sort of person I am. I have my full share of faults."

"They are the sort of faults I would gladly endure," Roger said gallantly. "And let me also warn you about Barnabas in another respect. He is not the marrying kind."

"Oh?" She pretended surprise.

"Not at all," Roger said emphatically. "He has broken the heart of more than one fine girl that I've known about. And there must be many others of whom I haven't heard. Don't let him lead you on."

"I will be on my guard," she promised.

"And don't shut yourself up in that old house," Roger said. "Come over here as often as you like. Elizabeth will welcome the company and I would value the opportunity of getting to know you better."

"But you must be busy at the plant in the daytime," she said.

Roger nodded. "I do have full days. In recent years I've expanded the business a great deal. Still, you could have Elizabeth bring you there to see me at work. I'd enjoy giving you a tour of the place."

"I'll keep it in mind," she promised.

"Remember all that I have said," Roger urged her.

As he finished speaking a middle-aged woman in a maid's uniform came into the room and told him he was wanted on the phone. Roger excused himself and went out to take the message. Adele joined Elizabeth and Barnabas.

Elizabeth smiled at her. "Barnabas has been telling me what a well-known person you are in the London modeling world. What a fascinating career!"

"I hope to return to it soon," she said.

"You must find it dreadfully dull in this small village," Elizabeth said.

"No," Adele told her. "It's an exciting change. I've never been in America before. And Barnabas makes a fine guide."

"I hope you have no more health setbacks," Elizabeth said sympathetically.

"The main thing is that she continue to let Doctor Hoffman check on her regularly and treat her as she feels necessary," Barnabas told his cousin.

"Julia is a fine doctor," Elizabeth agreed.

Adele glanced toward the living room door in time to see Roger come striding back in. It took her only a moment to note his pallor and the angry expression on his square face. He came straight to them and directed himself to Barnabas.

"I've had a most disturbing phone message," he said.

Barnabas took it calmly. "Indeed?"

"Yes," Roger said in an outraged manner. "From the Ellsworth police. It seems that the proprietor of a tavern there was attacked on the way from his place of business to his adjoining home. He was clawed and bitten by a weird greenish-gray animal which he insists looked like a wolf. Further, he says that when he first heard something behind him he turned and saw that it was a customer who'd been in his lounge. Someone he'd had a quarrel with. And as the man pounced on him, he changed into this bizarre animal!"

Barnabas smiled thinly. "It sounds as if this tavern owner might have been sampling too much of his own liquor."

Roger scowled. "The police don't think he was drunk. In fact, he doesn't drink at all. They called me to ask if Quentin were in the area since the description of the animal suggested a werewolf."

Elizabeth showed dismay. "They're not about to start that nonsense again."

"It's not nonsense," Roger snapped. "And you should know it."

Barnabas said, "Did they describe this fellow who is supposed to have turned into a wolf in the flash of a second?"

"Roughly. From what they said he was some sort of mulatto or Indian. He had brown skin and a shaven head and golden circlets in his ears."

Barnabas raised his eyebrows. "That doesn't sound much like the good-looking, curly-haired young man I know as my cousin Quentin."

Roger gave him a disdainful glance. "Quentin is a master of disguise, and you know it as well as I do."

"I'm sure there is an explanation for what happened," Elizabeth said with annoyance. "Probably the tavern keeper saw that man and then a dog as well. Some wild dog has attacked him and he has hopelessly confused the entire incident. It is unfair to bring up that ignorant village fable of a werewolf whenever anything of this sort takes place."

Roger said, "Dear sister, it was the police who called. One

doesn't tell the police they are ignorant and superstitious."

"I would have," Elizabeth said indignantly.

"Then you can answer them if they call again," Roger replied tartly.

"I wouldn't be upset about it," Barnabas advised. "I agree with the explanation Elizabeth offered. The tavern owner was obviously frightened and muddled."

"Let us hope so," Roger said grimly. "I can promise you I'll have some questions to ask Quentin if he shows up here."

"He won't come here," Elizabeth said, her lovely face angry. "He knows too well how you feel toward him."

"What do you expect?" Roger demanded. "Am I the only one who has any family pride?"

Barnabas said pointedly, "Doesn't family pride include a defense of all the family unless they are proven guilty?"

Roger's stern face showed an uneasy confusion. "I can do without your lectures on family behavior," he said curtly. "They'd be more welcome if you always conducted yourself in an exemplary manner."

"That would be expecting too much," Barnabas chided him with some amusement. "And what must Adele be thinking of all this talk and family in-fighting?"

She smiled wanly. "Please don't worry about me."

"I'm sorry, Adele," Roger Collins said, turning to her. "I didn't intend to cause this unhappy scene. But you can realize from it the strain my position as head of the family entails."

"Roger excites far too easily," Elizabeth said reproachfully. "Quentin is a fine person and I will not have strangers recklessly accusing him."

Barnabas gave Adele a significant glance. "I'm afraid it is time we went back to the house. You remember what Doctor Hoffman said about your getting plenty of rest."

"It seems you both just got here!" Roger protested.

"It's been longer than that," she smiled at the quick-tempered man. "And I am weary. So I'll say good night if you don't mind."

Roger and Elizabeth saw them to the door. And Roger was most insistent that Adele return for dinner the following night. She promised to consider it and then she and Barnabas went out into the cold winter night.

A pale silver moon lit up the snowy fields and ice-covered trees and fences and made a scene of magic beauty. They strolled side by side with arms linked.

"What about Quentin?" she asked as soon as they were alone.

He shrugged. "It must have been him."

"Why would he do such a thing?"

"We'll have to wait to ask him before we know that," Barnabas said.

"If they only guessed that he was in the area and going to stay here with you," she said.

"Let's hope Roger doesn't find out. Elizabeth is all right."

"Roger is a very strange person," she agreed. "Before all the excitement he spent most of his time warning me about you and practically proposing to me."

"Bravo!" Barnabas laughed. "I had no idea he'd be so bold."

"I had to fight myself to keep from telling him I was also one of the living dead. It would have been worth it just to see the expression on his face."

"He wouldn't have believed you," Barnabas promised her. "He'd have blamed me for corrupting you into lying on my behalf. That's the way his brain works. He closes his mind to anything he doesn't agree with."

"In that he's not alone."

Barnabas halted along the narrow path in the snow and asked her, "Do you mind if we take a short detour before we go back to the old house?"

"No."

"Good," he said. "I want to show you Widows' Hill." And he went on to tell her the tragic history of the hill. And of the suicides who'd jumped from the high point of the cliffs to their deaths.

They reached the point of land overlooking Collinsport Bay and she was able to set the sweeping beam of the lighthouse which marked Collinsport Point on the right and the myriad of twinkling white lights which showed the village on the left.

"I often come here to be alone and think of other times," Barnabas said, his handsome face sad.

"You've seen so much happen here over the years," she said, studying him with sympathy. "Is Collinwood the haunted place which Elizabeth suggested?"

He nodded. "Yes. That house hides many secrets in its forty rooms."

"And ghosts?"

"And ghosts," he agreed. "Every old mansion has its ghosts. They are more restless in the shadowed corridors of Collinwood than in most places."

She gave him a wry look. "We two are phantoms if it comes to that."

He glanced at her strangely. "True. And for the first time I am not alone in that state here. You share the experience with me. It makes it so much easier to bear, I'm almost lighthearted."

Her eyes met his with tenderness in them. "I've been

thinking."

"What?"

"Perhaps my meeting Stefan Spivak and undergoing that operation wasn't as tragic as I at first thought."

Barnabas was baffled. "How can you believe that?"

"The operation made me one of the living dead and brought me to meet you."

"So?"

"So why try to be cured?" she said. "I'm content with my fate if I can go on being with you."

Barnabas frowned. "You mustn't say such things. Julia has to find a cure for you!"

"Even if I don't want it?"

Barnabas took her by the arms. "Even if you don't want it! Even if it means my losing you! And don't think that will be easy for me now that I've grown used to having you with me."

She looked up at him with anguish. "I'm willing to remain with you always! Don't you care for me at all, Barnabas?"

"It is because I care for you I can't condemn you to such an existence," he told her.

"I love you, Barnabas," she said.

He drew her close to him and kissed her gently on the lips. After holding her for a long moment he sighed and said, "Time to go back."

She clung to his arm. "Think about what I've said, Barnabas."

He shook his head. "Only if everything else fails. Only if Julia is not able to do anything for you."

"I don't care any longer."

They started back, his arm around her. He said, "You mustn't feel that way. My greatest happiness would be to restore you to normalcy."

"And I'd lose you," she said. "What life will I have to return to?"

"Your career."

"It's not all that important to me."

"And this Douglas Edwards you've spoken of," Barnabas said. "I'll wager that young man is still very much in love with you."

"I turned him away."

"All the more reason he'd be glad to hear from you again," Barnabas said.

"I'm not sure I love him any longer," she said. "I know I'm in love with you."

Barnabas pressed her close to him as they walked on and in a teasing voice asked, "What about Roger? There's a prospect for you. He asked you to think about marrying him."

"You're joking!" she protested. "He's far too old!"

"And about a hundred and thirty years younger than I am," he reminded her mockingly.

"Those years don't count since you haven't aged!"

"They are written on my mind," Barnabas warned her solemnly.

In a few minutes they had reached the old house. It was all very quiet as they went inside.

"Did Roger complain about your living here?" he asked.

"He's very upset about it," she said with a smile. "You knew he would be."

"He spoke to me about it," Barnabas agreed. "I had an idea he wouldn't let the subject drop."

They went on down the shadowed hall to the living room and as they entered the candlelit room a familiar figure with brown skin, a shaven head and golden circlets in his ears, stood there to welcome them. The errant Quentin Collins!

CHAPTER 9

"I thought you two would never arrive," Quentin Collins told them. He was completely at ease with a satisfied look on his face.

Barnabas confronted him with, "What were you up to in Ellsworth?"

"Ellsworth?" Quentin repeated mildly.

"Don't pretend innocence," Barnabas warned him. "We were at Collinwood a little while ago when Roger got a phone call about you."

"Really?" Quentin said. "News travels fast."

Adele could see that the young man in the weird make-up wasn't in the least upset. And she wondered just what had been his role in the escapade and if he would tell them about it.

Barnabas said, "If I'm to have you here I think I'm at least entitled to an explanation."

Quentin gave her a wondering smile. "Do you think Barnabas is behaving in a cousinly way?"

"I think you should tell us what happened," she said. "Roger was very upset."

"I can imagine," Quentin said. "What was his version of the story?"

"The police called him and told him that a tavern keeper had been attacked by a man who'd changed into a wolf. They had to send him to the hospital, he was so torn up. The police wanted to know if you were at Collinwood. Apparently the man had babbled about a werewolf."

"I'm flattered by their interest," Quentin said. "The tavern keeper happens to be a rogue and a bully. I sat in his place and watched him steal from and then beat up one of his drunken customers. It struck me that he needed a lesson. So I waited until he closed the place and was on his way home. Then I approached him."

"So you did attack him!" Barnabas said.

"I gave him a slight roughing up," Quentin admitted. "All that talk of my becoming a wolf was sheer imagination on his part."

"I wonder, Barnabas said. "It seems to me you picked a poor time to assume the role of Don Quixote."

"I didn't expect to return to that tavern," Quentin said. "I had to seek that fellow out then or not at all."

"Not at all would have been smarter," Barnabas snapped.

Quentin looked amused. "I seem to recall some rather dramatic moves on your part to right wrongs. Why complain so when I try to do the same thing?"

"You don't have any judgment," Barnabas complained.

Quentin turned to Adele and said, "Surely you don't agree with my cousin in this, do you?"

She smiled wanly. "It's difficult for me to offer an opinion. You may have meted out justice to the tavern keeper, but at the same time you placed yourself in danger."

"A familiar position for me," he assured her. "Now that I've seen you two and discussed this, I'm going to bid you both good night. I don't have your facility for sleeping in the daytime."

Barnabas gave him a warning glance. "If you bring the police here it could be bad for all of us. Especially for Adele."

Quentin asked, "Did Roger tell the police I might be in the district?"

"No. He said you weren't here," Barnabas replied. "In that case they'll not likely make a trip out this far. It is mid-winter. And I'll promise not to excite their interest again."

"I'll depend on that," Barnabas informed him.

"You can, cousin," Quentin said pleasantly. "I'll also keep a watch here with Willie in the daytime just in case." He bowed to Adele. "Good night, Adele. Most delightful experience meeting you." And he left them and went upstairs.

After he left, Barnabas sighed and said, "I hope we're not in for a lot of complications and trouble."

They sat through the winter night talking before the fireplace until the logs burned to gray ashes and the last hint of flame vanished. Barnabas told her of the legend of the Phantom Mariner and how it was said that any who saw him were doomed to death. She listened to him, thrilling with excitement. And then, all at once, it was near dawn. Time for them to part and go to their respective rooms for their long daylight sleep.

Barnabas kissed her a fond good night and she went up to her room. The thought of him stretched out in that gray casket in the dark cellar below filled her with sadness. If only Dr. Hoffman could cure them both. But would that be a solution? If Barnabas was cured, she was sure that the woman doctor would be ready to marry him. It seemed no matter which way it went, Adele was doomed to lose the love of the handsome man.

The familiar sleepiness came to her. She closed her eyes and gradually the normal world slipped away from her. When she woke up from the dreamless sleep it was dusk. After a while she got up from the bed and readied herself to go downstairs.

When she went down she found Barnabas in a serious conversation with Quentin. The men rose to greet her as she joined them and Barnabas said, "A most amazing thing has happened."

"What?" she asked.

"Quentin was in the village for a little this afternoon," Barnabas said. "And he has brought back some information which puzzles me."

"Explain, don't talk all around it," the shaven-headed Quentin complained.

"Very well," Barnabas said. He turned to her. "A woman whose name is familiar to me has come to the village and bought an old mansion. And she's already opened it and is living there. She's hired local workers to do a lot of repairs and make changes in the place. According to rumor, it's to be some sort of hotel."

Adele was surprised. "I can't imagine why anyone would open a hotel here in winter!"

"Nor anyone else," Barnabas said bitterly.

Quentin suggested, "Perhaps she's starting early to have it ready for the summer trade."

"It could be that," Adele said.

Barnabas appeared troubled. "I think not. This woman is not the type to operate a hotel. She's a former stage star of both New York and London. Lately I've heard stories that she's had little work. And also other rumors of a darker nature."

"Go on," Adele urged him.

Barnabas gave her a strange look. "I have heard that she became a vampire. And that she went to Stefan Spivak to be cured. And in payment for his helping her she'd become a member of his staff."

Fear raced through Adele. "She's connected with Spivak?"

"There's a chance of it," Barnabas said. "Her name is Olivia Warner and she has a mad, middle-aged brother. Not insane enough for hospitalization but definitely an eccentric. His name is Anton. It seems that he is here with her. So it has to be the same Olivia Warner."

"What would bring her here?" Adele worried.

"I wish I knew," Barnabas said. "Perhaps she heard that I spend a good deal of my time here."

Her heart was pounding. "Could it be because of me? That Spivak is angry with you for helping me get away from him. And he's sent this woman here to work some evil against us?"

"Don't jump to any conclusions," Barnabas said. "Let us have Quentin try to pick up some more information. The woman's being here may have nothing to do with Spivak at all."

Quentin said, "I agree. Don't worry until I get a few more facts."

But she did worry. She tried to hide it from Barnabas and the others but all the panic she'd felt during those terrible days and nights when she'd been a virtual prisoner in the gray old castle in Switzerland came back to plague her. She was filled with a certainty that this sinister Olivia Warner had come to Collinsport in pursuit of her. That the woman had come to the remote village to seek revenge from her and perhaps to destroy Barnabas as well!

She tried to think of some special reason for the former stage star showing up there in mid-winter. And she began to feel that it might have something to do with the operation. Perhaps it had gone wrong in some way so that Countess Dario, whom she'd known as Lisa, was slowly going back to her former state of one of the living dead. In that case it might be Olivia Warner's purpose to seek out Adele as Lisa's opposite and take her back to Stefan Spivak for another operation. Or perhaps to try a more direct method, by simply causing her death!

Adele was haunted by both these fears. Either kidnapping or death! At the same time Barnabas kept her away from the village and refused to think there was any connection between her and the arrival of Olivia Warner. It was a trying time!

There were the drives to Dr. Julia Hoffman's clinic, with only negative results. The woman continued to supply both Adele and Barnabas with the serum to assuage their need for blood, but that was all she seemed to be able to do.

On the most recent visit Dr. Hoffman had sat with Adele across her desk in the neat white-walled office on the ground floor of the hospital, while Barnabas waited outside.

The attractive woman doctor gave Adele a searching look. "I've noticed that you've not been so worried about my curing you in these last few weeks," she observed.

"I'm not so concerned any longer," she admitted.

"I find that strange," Julia said. "Are you resigned to being one of the living dead?"

"In a way."

Julia Hoffman frowned. "Just what does that mean?"

She hesitated. "If there's no hope of a cure, it's useless for me to go on dreaming about one."

"Oh?"

"No. I may as well accept my condition."

The woman doctor looked wise. "Especially since Barnabas is in the same boat with you?"

"That has helped."

"You must have an idea of how precarious a condition you're both in," Julia Hoffman said. "You know what the thirst for blood is like."

"Only too well," she said quietly.

"If I run short of the serum I've been giving you," the doctor said with a solemn look on her attractive face, "you'll go back to that demented state where the need for blood is stronger than anything else."

"I know."

Julia Hoffman sat back in her chair. "Or if I should just decide to cut off your supply of serum without any reason? What then?"

She stared at the woman in white. "You wouldn't!"

"I might," Julia Hoffman said in a tense voice. And she got up and took a few steps across the room before she turned to say, "You're in love with Barnabas, aren't you?"

There was no point in lying. Julia would see through any protest she might make. So she said in a small voice, "Yes. I do love him."

Julia looked suddenly weary. "I thought so."

"I'm sorry," Adele looked down. "I know you love him too."

"But that didn't stop you from allowing yourself to become involved with him," the woman doctor said bitterly.

Adele looked up at her with plaintive eyes. "It wasn't anything I wanted to happen."

"Does he love you?"

"In a way."

Julia Hoffman said angrily, "Either he loves you or he doesn't. You say he does. So while I keep you two in a state of comparative ease this nasty deceit is going on behind my back."

"You make it sound as if Barnabas and I were plotting against you!" she exclaimed. "That's not true!"

"If there is a romance going on between you, where does that leave me?" Julia wanted to know.

"It's not in any way as you picture it," Adele protested.

The woman doctor sighed and came back behind her desk. She stood there with a troubled look on her attractive face. "All this time I've been in love with Barnabas and have devoted myself to trying to help save him. And it only took you to come along to make him forget me."

Adele jumped up. "Be fair! The romance between you had been called off or at least suspended before I ever came here! Barnabas told me that!"

Julia said, "You'll never take him from me permanently. I won't let that happen. I warn you!"

"What do you mean?"

"Just what I've told you."

"Is that a threat against me? Against Barnabas?" she worried.

"Think about it," the woman doctor said quietly. "I won't be discussing this with you again."

"Very well," she said. "I'll ask Barnabas not to bring me here any more."

"But he will," Julia Hoffman predicted. "And I'll continue in my efforts to cure you."

There was a knock on the door of the private office and Julia called out for whoever it was to enter. The door opened and a stout, pompous man in a dark suit presented himself.

"I trust I'm not intruding, Doctor," the man said.

"Not at all, we'd just finished our discussion," Dr. Julia Hoffman said. "I'd like you to meet Miss Adele Marriot, Professor Stokes."

The professor beamed. "Of course. I've heard all about you. I've been doing special tests on your blood. We haven't found the answer to your trouble yet but I'm hopeful."

"Thank you," Adele said, grateful for his arrival. The situation had grown tense between her and Julia.

Professor Stokes said, "I think we could accomplish more if you remained in the hospital. But Mr. Collins says that is not possible."

"It's not convenient," she said.

"Well, in that case we'll just have to proceed a little more slowly," the pompous man said. "But you mustn't lose courage. The prospects are quite good."

"I'll see you on your way," Julia Hoffman said to Adele. And after thanking Professor Stokes again, Adele left the office with her.

In the waiting room Barnabas rose with an air of impatience. "I wondered if anything had gone wrong," he said. "You're later than usual."

Dr. Hoffman gave Adele a significant look. "We had some things to discuss. Matters we don't generally get to. Everything went well. I'm going to have a session with Professor Stokes regarding Adele's blood factor now. We'll expect her on Friday night at the usual time."

Barnabas said, "Elizabeth wants to know when you're going to pay a visit to Collinwood."

"Sometime soon," the woman doctor said with a thin smile. "Remember me to her."

It was well after midnight as she and Barnabas began the drive back to Collinwood. They made it a point not to leave late following the close call they'd had the dawn they'd come upon the road block. As Adele sat beside the man she loved, she kept hearing over and over again the quiet threat Julia had made. The woman doctor had promised she would never allow her to take Barnabas from her.

After a few minutes Barnabas gave her a quick glance. "What is wrong? You've been terribly quiet since we left the clinic."

"It's nothing."

"I know better."

"Nothing to bother you about then," she said wearily.

"Let me be the judge of that," Barnabas insisted, his handsome face grim.

"Julia accused me of being in love with you."

There was a strained moment of silence broken only by the humming of the car's engine. Then he said, "Why should she do that?"

"She simply brought it up. Accused us of being lovers."

"I do happen to be fond of you," he said. "I make no apologies for that."

"I tried to explain how it was with us," she said. "She didn't understand. And she became angry. It was dreadful. I don't want to go back to her again."

"We must," he said, his eyes on the road ahead. "If only for the serum."

"She mentioned that and threatened to withdraw it."

"She won't. She's too much the scientist to destroy any experiment, and you are an important experimental case for her and Professor Stokes."

She cried unhappily, "But I don't want to be in her debt!"

"You needn't feel that you are," he said. "The best thing you can do is forget the whole conversation. She'll do the same by the time you see her again."

"I wouldn't count on it," Adele warned him. And she meant it. She felt he was being much too optimistic. She had seen Julia's anger and knew it had been real.

In the days that followed tensions grew higher at Collinwood. There were other reported sightings of a werewolf. Quentin denied any responsibility for them. And Adele was inclined to agree with him that these additional reportings of werewolves were the result of overtaxed imaginations.

And then a worse blow fell. A clamor rose when a young woman employed by the hotel was attacked while walking home from work late at night. She was found unconscious on the road by a passing motorist who discovered marks of vampire fangs on her throat. By bad luck Adele and Barnabas had gone over to visit at Collinwood, unaware of the attack.

When they went into the living room Roger Collins came at Barnabas in a fury. He briefly told him what had taken place and with a fiery gleam in his eyes asked him to explain.

"Explain what?" Barnabas said.

Roger snapped, "Why you attacked that girl?"

Elizabeth, who had been hovering in the background, now came up beside her brother and told him, "It's not fair to accuse Barnabas that way. And in front of Adele!"

Roger wasn't to be silenced. "Better she find out the sort of person he is," he said.

Barnabas said calmly, "What you've told me is the first I've heard of the attack. Someone else was responsible and I'll make it my business to try and find out who it was."

"That sounds like a weak alibi," Roger said scornfully. "I know what has gone on here in the past. You've been behaving yourself too long."

"I won't argue about it," Barnabas said tautly. And he turned to her. "Are you leaving with me, Adele?"

"Yes," she said. And she gave Roger a cool look. "Good night," she said. "I think you should be careful with your accusations if you're out to protect your family name."

She and Barnabas went back to the old house for a conference with Quentin. The three of them sat before the fireplace in the candle lit living room discussing what might have gone on.

Barnabas looked angry. "I know who we have to blame."

"Who?" she asked worriedly.

"You should be able to guess," he said. "That Olivia Warner

or her mad brother, Anton. We know that they both were of the living dead. And I'm not sure she's cured. Certainly the brother didn't have Stefan Spivak's operation. So it could be him."

Quentin nodded his shaven head. "It's more than likely. The house they bought is only down the lane from the hotel. And it was in that area the girl was attacked."

"I've got to do something about this," Barnabas said, rising. "I'm going to drive into town and make some inquiries."

Adele also got to her feet. "You'd better be careful. I don't think you should show yourself in the village. Not with a lot of them believing you were responsible for the attack."

"If I don't show myself they'll decide I'm afraid," he pointed out. "I can't win no matter which way it goes."

Quentin told him, "There's truth in what Adele says. Let it rest for a night or two."

"Until there are more attacks?" Barnabas said. "I can't do that. I'm going into the village now."

"Let me go along," she said.

"No," Barnabas told her. "You stay here with Quentin. I'll be back in an hour or so."

"Don't be longer," she begged. "I'll be worrying about you every minute."

He left right away. She and Quentin began the vigil until his return. She had somber forebodings about his going to the village. She feared she might never see him again. She was convinced the presence of Olivia Warner in the village indicated there was an evil conspiracy forming under the direction of the sinister Stefan Spivak.

Quentin was standing before the fireplace. He told her, "Don't look so gloomy. Barnabas can take care of himself."

"I wonder," she said.

"I've never known him not to be able to," was his cousin's reply.

"There are so many in the village against him," she worried.

"Against me as well."

"But you've been keeping away from Collinsport lately," she pointed out.

"I go in occasionally but I don't make myself more conspicuous than I can help, though this disguise has turned into a liability rather than an asset," he said with some disgust.

"Roger still doesn't guess you're staying here."

"Blame the cold weather and his lack of curiosity for his not coming up here to find out," Quentin said with a smile on his brown-skinned face.

Making an effort to get her mind off her troubles, she returned his smile and said, "I suspect you're handsome without all the make-up."

"And with my hair," he said ruefully. "Don't forget this disguise cost me a full head of brown curly hair and sideburns."

"What a difference they would make," she said.

He nodded. "I wanted to make myself seem a completely different person. I managed. But now I'm so different I still attract too much attention. But so far no one in the village has recognized me as Quentin."

"So the disguise is actually a success."

"In a stupid sort of way," Quentin said.

They talked of his travels and where he planned to go in the summer ahead. He had a tour of Germany and the Scandinavian countries in mind. He'd been there before and she also knew some of the places. They forgot about the passing time as they became interested in comparing experiences. Then she was suddenly aware that it was after two o'clock and Barnabas hadn't returned.

Jumping up, she exclaimed, "Something is wrong!"

"Doesn't have to be," he said, trying to placate her.

"I can't go on waiting and worrying," she declared, "Let us take your car and go in to the village."

"He may be on his way back here," Quentin suggested.

"There's only one road plowed," she said. "If he is heading back we'll meet him on the way. And if he isn't we should try and find out why."

"How?"

"We'll look for his car for a start. It isn't all that large a village. We should be able to find it."

Quentin sighed. "I see there's no arguing with you."

She gave him a forthright look. "If you're afraid to go I'll risk it on my own."

He showed annoyance. "You know I'm not afraid. Put on your coat and we'll go."

They let Willie know they were leaving and set out in the small car. It drove more roughly than the one Barnabas owned and its headlights bounced their beam up and down as they raced over the rutted road. As she feared, there was no sign of Barnabas returning.

She sat braced against the seat to endure the jolting. "Something has gone wrong," she said.

"Don't worry," Quentin begged her as he drove the tiny car.

They reached the main highway and the going was easier, but she was becoming increasingly depressed. It seemed certain Barnabas had come to some harm.

"We must get him safely back to the house before dawn," she reminded Quentin.

Quentin gave her a troubled glance. "You also have your problems with the dawn."

"I'm also one of the living dead," she said grimly. "Your curse is not nearly so restricting."

"But rather more shocking when it happens," Quentin said in a quieter voice.

"Sorry," she told him. "I wasn't trying to make it seem you had no serious problems."

"It's all right," he said. "We'll soon be in the village. You better start keeping an eye open for his car."

"I will," she promised.

They reached the steep incline of the main street, which was deserted and dark except for the few street lamps.

They passed the hotel and Quentin took the lane down by it. It was plowed wide enough for two cars to pass with banks of snow on either side of it. Ahead there was a house outlined against the dark winter sky with several lights showing from small windows on the top floor.

Quentin said, "There's the house Olivia Warner and her brother have."

"Look!" Adele cried. "I see the car in that driveway." And the car Barnabas drove was parked in the driveway of another small house in which all the lights were out.

Quentin braked his small car to a halt. "I'd better get out and see if I can find him."

She glanced fearfully in the direction of the big house with the lights at attic level. "He must be in there. Either spying on them or trapped by them."

"I don't see Barnabas easily trapped," Quentin said. "You wait in the car. I'll scout around and see what I can find out."

"Let me go with you!"

"Not a chance," Quentin told her as he got out. "You stay here."

So she remained in the front seat of the small car as he vanished in the darkness. One moment she caught a glimpse of him against the snowbank and in the next he was gone. She had an overwhelming impulse to turn on the car headlights to try and follow his progress. But she knew this would only hinder him. So she sat in the shadows and trembled.

CHAPTER 10

The waiting went on. Her fears increased the longer Quentin was gone. At last she felt she could stand it no longer, so she opened the car door and got out. Then she started along the snow-covered road in the same direction which Quentin had taken. She felt sure that in a moment she'd catch up with him. But as she went deeper in the shadowed quiet of the side road, there was still no sign of his tall figure.

At last she reached the great house which had been purchased by the mysterious Olivia Warner and her brother. She noticed that all the lights in the attic but one had been turned off. She was standing in the shadow of the big house debating on this when she heard a footstep behind her. In the next instant a powerful hand was clamped across her mouth and an arm seized her around the waist and literally lifted her off her feet.

She tried to scream out and couldn't. She fought back savagely and yet was unable to free herself. Her captor seemed impervious to her struggling as he dragged her down a slippery flight of stone steps and then dodged into a dark cave-like entrance in the side of the building's foundation. From there she was dragged across a rough surface in the darkness. And it was then she fainted.

When she opened her eyes she was in a large sparsely

furnished room, with a single lamp glowing on a round table beside an easy chair. In the easy chair was the most enormous woman she had ever seen whose square face sported three jowls. She had bulging, ugly blue eyes and dyed red hair of a brilliant color with a sparkling bangle gracing it.

The fat woman grasped the arms of her chair and her bosom trembled beneath the green dress she wore as she gave a raucous laugh. "So you decided to attend my party, Miss Marriot."

Adele raised herself on an elbow, aching all over from her struggles. "What do you mean having me dragged here this way?"

"Was Anton rough with you? That's too bad!" The fat woman's tone was mocking. She eyed the darkness somewhere beyond Adele and said, "I'm shocked at your behavior, dear brother!" And she laughed again.

From out of the shadows emerged an apparition that was all too familiar to Adele. The massive giant she'd seen back at the clinic in Switzerland. The mindless monster whom she'd spied on from the shadows in fear. He glared at her with his insane eyes and uttered a growling sound.

Adele sprang to her feet and moved closer to the fat woman. Staring at her, she said, "You're Olivia Warner."

"You recognize your hostess! How nice!" The fat woman mocked her.

She gazed at the monster over her shoulder. "And that is your brother, Anton. I saw him at the clinic in Switzerland."

"What an excellent memory you have," the fat woman said, her jowls wobbling as she spoke. "Dear Anton was a patient at the clinic. And they saved him from the living death. What a wonderful man Doctor Spivak is."

"He's a charlatan who harmed me to cure someone like your brother!"

"Come now," Olivia Warner reproved her with a jeweled, pudgy finger. "You mustn't say such things about your betters!"

"What do you want with me?" Adele demanded, fear and anger clamoring within her.

"A good question," the fat woman said. And she glanced toward the monster again. "Have you any suggestions, Anton?"

The monstrous Anton grinned and his thick lips parted to reveal almost toothless gums. He growled again like some kind of animal.

Olivia Warner gave her attention to Adele again. "Anton has a rather narrow range of conversation but it is vivid, don't you agree? I have the impression he doesn't care for you."

"I demand that you let me leave here!" Adele cried.

The fat woman moved in her chair and it creaked under her enormous weight. "I would like to do that," she said agreeably. "Nothing would please me better, dear Miss Marriot. But unfortunately that is beyond me. There are others interested in you."

"What have you done to Barnabas and Quentin?"

The fat woman looked surprised. "Barnabas and Quentin? I haven't seen either of them. Though I know them by reputation. Scoundrels both if what the villagers say is only half-true."

"They are not scoundrels," she argued. "And they must be in here somewhere."

"You're mistaken," Olivia Warner told her. "This house isn't all that easy to enter. We made an exception with you."

Adele glanced around the big, dark room. "I'll find a way out," she said defiantly.

"You may if you're willing to try to escape with every bone in your arms and legs broken. Anton thoroughly enjoys snapping bones. I have only to clap my hands and he'll start on you." The fat woman lifted her hands as if she were about to clap them and the monstrous Anton came a step closer to Adele and snarled more loudly this time.

"Don't come near me!" Adele cried and drew away.

"You're annoying him," the fat woman warned her. "You're taking a dreadful risk."

"What is it you want of me?" she demanded helplessly.

"Your opposite in the operation needs to see you," Olivia Warner told her.

"You mean Lisa, the Countess Dario?"

"No, I do not," the fat woman said, smiling at her maliciously. "Though she may be here soon."

"Who, then?"

"You'll find out!" was the mocking reply. But Adele was certain the fat woman was lying, and that Lisa had been her opposite.

Adele said, "I want nothing to do with you or anything connected with Doctor Spivak!"

"It seems you would rather battle with Anton," the stout woman said with a sigh. "I'll have to get him to lock you up until the others join me if you aren't more considerate of what you have to say!"

She found herself caught between the fat woman and her monstrous brother. Changing her tactics, she begged tearfully, "Please don't keep me here against my will."

"No harm will come to you," the fat woman said, leaning forward in the easy chair so that her massive, jowled face was highlighted by the table lamp. A face remarkable in its ferocity!

"I can promise you that!" It was the voice of Barnabas which rang out in the big room, and a moment later he appeared in the shadows at the side of the massive Anton. And in his hands were the most peculiar weapons she'd ever seen, a mallet and a thin black stake with a pointed end.

The fat woman rose from her chair, dark with rage. "What do you want in here?"

"I'll chance a stake through your brother's heart if you don't care to release this girl," Barnabas said sternly.

The giant hadn't moved an inch but stood there glaring at Barnabas. It seemed that he might spring at him any moment. But Barnabas was keeping him in full view and apparently ready to deal with him.

"We will not tolerate violence," the fat woman complained.

"What did you use to bring that girl in here?" Barnabas wanted to know.

"I merely wanted to chat with her for a little," the fat woman said, a hint of a whine in her voice betraying her. The sight of Barnabas had struck fear into her.

And then to clinch the frightened moment, Quentin appeared from a murky doorway and came in the darkness to the other side of the giant. In his hand was a gun.

He brandished it at Anton and said, "We can manage this nicely." Anton growled and looked uneasily in his sister's direction.

"Don't hurt him!" she cried and waddled across to stand protectively before the giant man. It would have been humorous under other conditions but there was nothing humorous about it now.

Barnabas said, "We'll just keep your brother as hostage as we make our exit from the house."

"You mustn't!" the fat woman begged. "You mustn't harm him in any way."

"Just let us get out of here!" Barnabas said impatiently.

"Keep that heathen away from my brother!" Olivia Warner screamed.

Quentin came and took Adele's arm. "I know a shortcut," he told her.

"Barnabas?" She jerked her head toward the man in the caped coat.

"He'll manage," Quentin said impatiently. "Let's go!"

And under his guidance she finally managed to make her escape.

At last they were in the cold open air. She turned to him.

"What about Barnabas?" she worried.

Quentin glanced into the darkness of the house through the door from which they'd just escaped. "Here comes Barnabas or someone," he said, as he raised his gun again, ready to use it.

But it was Barnabas who finally came rushing out and so Quentin let the gun drop to a relaxed position once again. "How are you?" Quentin demanded.

"No time for that now," Barnabas said, pushing both of them forward. "Anton may decide to battle it with us down here. Let's go fast!"

The three of them raced along the snow-covered road to reach their cars. Barnabas grasped her by the arm and shouted to Quentin, "I'll take her with me!" And then he hastily shoved her into his car.

In a moment they had backed out onto the roadway and were heading for Collinwood once more with Quentin in the small car behind them. She sat back with a deep sigh as soon as she knew they were safe.

"That was a close call!" she said.

Barnabas's handsome face showed strain. "What made you follow me to the village?"

"We were worried about you."

"There was no need."

"How could I be sure of that?" she wanted to know.

"At least Quentin shouldn't have left you alone."

"It wasn't his fault," she said. "I got out of the car to follow him. I'd likely have been all right if I'd stayed where he left me."

Barnabas gave her a troubled glance as they drove along. "It could have ended very differently for you. You were virtually the prisoner of that mad old woman and her brother."

"She intended to keep me there. She spoke of others coming."

"Good news!" Barnabas said grimly.

"I thought something had happened to you. It was wonderful when you made an appearance as you did. I could tell at once Olivia Warner was afraid of you."

"I hoped she might be."

"And her brother is such a mad monster he doesn't think for himself. He depends on her for his instructions. He was at the clinic in Switzerland. I'm sure he was a patient."

"I don't doubt it," Barnabas said. "Olivia has put on a lot of weight since her stage days."

She looked around to see out of the rear window of the car. And the lights of Quentin's car emerged around a turn in the road as she watched. "Quentin's still with us," she said in a relieved voice.

"We have some talking to do when we get home," Barnabas commented.

They turned into the private road leading to Collinwood. The great mansion was in complete darkness as they passed it. And within a few minutes they were parking beside the old brick house and she and Barnabas were standing in the cold night air waiting for Quentin to get out of his car and join them on the steps.

Quentin hurried along the walk and up the steps with a smile on his face. "We could have had a lot more fun back there if we'd not been bogged down by having to rescue Adele."

"Sorry," she said. "I didn't realize I was such a nuisance."

"Don't pay any attention to him," Barnabas warned her as they entered the old house together.

They were all standing in the living room with the soft light of the candles on the fireplace mantel providing the only illumination for the big room.

Looking especially noble in the candlelight, Barnabas said, "Olivia Warner and her brother attacked Adele and had intentions of kidnapping her."

Quentin regarded him with a mocking smile on his pleasant face. "What have you in mind, Cousin Barnabas? Shall we make a charge against them? Can't you picture two vampires and a werewolf solemnly entering the Ellsworth Police Station and asking that the police arrest those two with attempted kidnapping?"

Adele sighed, "Quentin is right. We can't ask the law for help."

Barnabas frowned. "Then we may have to make our own law and punishment."

"What did you find in the house tonight?" Quentin asked.

Barnabas eyed them both solemnly. "I made a thorough check of the place. The inside has been almost all altered. The workmen have cut one area up into a lot of small rooms like those in a hospital. In fact, I'd say the place has been converted into a kind of hospital."

Her eyes opened wide. "And that old woman said others were coming!"

"My guess is that Spivak is planning to set up an American branch of his notorious clinic here in Collinsport," Baranabas said.

"That fits in with what we've heard," Quentin remarked.

"Perhaps Spivak's luck has finally run out," Barnabas said. "He may be a fugitive from Switzerland and they're fixing up this spot for him here as a new headquarters."

"I think that's it," she agreed. "What can we do?"

"Not much at the moment," Quentin said. "We'd best wait

and see who does turn up here. Then we'll know how big a fight we have on our hands."

"I'm frightened," she said, studying the faces of the two men.

"It may turn out to be a difficult and unpleasant business," Barnabas was willing to admit. "You might be wise to follow Julia Hoffman's suggestion and spend some time at her hospital. It could help bring you to a cure quicker."

"No," she objected. "I want to remain here with you and Quentin."

"I hope you won't regret it," Barnabas said in a quiet voice.

"Of course she won't," Quentin said in his jovial way. "I prefer having her remain here with us."

"Even though she may be placed in a dangerous spot such as she was tonight?" Barnabas asked.

"You rescued me easily enough," she said.

"It might not be that easy again," he warned.

"It's only fair I should share any risks with you two," she said.

"You remember the reason I went into the village tonight," Barnabas reminded her. "There have been vampire attacks for which I was blamed."

"I know," she worried.

"Did you learn anything about them?" Quentin wanted to know.

"Yes," Barnabas said. "I'm sure that either Olivia or Anton Warner are of the living dead. Perhaps they are both vampires. But one of them made the attacks for which I was given the credit."

She said, "Is that why you came in with that mallet and pointed stake?"

"I brought the hawthorn and mallet to drive through Anton's heart and you saw how his sister tried to protect him. She didn't want him destroyed. So I'm certain he's a vampire."

"I agree," Adele worried.

"One of them made the attack on the village girls," Barnabas said.

Quentin nodded. "And they'll go on!"

"Worse attacks!" Barnabas said. "We've got to stand our ground and somehow drive them out of Collinsport. And we can't expect any help or understanding from the police, Roger, or any of the ordinary people of the village. We're in this strictly alone."

Adele looked at the two men with a forlorn smile. "Three outcasts of the night!"

Quentin said, "At least we've found a kind of comradeship. And we must keep it."

"I would prefer to have Adele out of it," Barnabas said. "But if she won't agree, there's nothing I can do."

"I won't go to stay with Julia Hoffman if that is what it would mean," Adele said. "Knowing how she feels about certain things, I can't."

Barnabas's face seemed more gaunt than usual. "Very well," he said. "We'll look to you, Quentin, to keep us informed on what takes place during the days. We can take care of the hours of darkness on our own. If we work together maybe we can stand up to this invasion threat of Spivak and his gang."

So it was arranged. They talked until dawn was showing in the sky and then Barnabas kissed her and they parted. She went to her room filled with fears and premonitions. She knew the power of Dr. Stefan Spivak. If he'd been chased out of his European retreat he'd be more anxious and desperate to make this new headquarters a success. If he were allowed to establish his evil clinic in Collinsport it would open up an entirely new phase of his career.

She stretched out on the bed in the shadowed room as the sleep of death slowly took hold of her. She was very confused. Maybe it would be easier if she and Barnabas simply fled. Quentin had no need to stay either. And she and Barnabas could find a sort of future somewhere as sharers of the vampire curse. They would always lurk in the shadows but at least they would have each other.

In the beginning she'd been revolted at the knowledge she was one of the living dead. But now she'd come to terms with it because of her love for Barnabas. Of course it was the serum which made the difference, the serum which Dr. Julia Hoffman was still able to offer them, and which kept them from the wild thirsting for blood which had tortured her until she was given the serum.

The frightening truth was that Dr. Julia Hoffman could withdraw the serum whenever she liked. Not that it was liable to happen, since Julia was in love with Barnabas. But it meant they were beholden to the woman doctor. This troubled Adele more than she cared to admit.

She also worried that Julia might devise some plan whereby one of them was cured and the other left in the vampire state. Julia might prefer to cure her to get her out of the way, while keeping Barnabas under the curse so that she would continue to have a hold on him. It was all a troublesome business climaxed now by the arrival of the eccentric Olivia Warner and her mad brother, Anton. If they were the vanguard of Spivak's complete entourage, as it seemed they could well be, then things were bound to be worse. With this grim conclusion Adele sank deep in sleep.

Dusk came and she went downstairs. Willie was passing through the hall as she came down, and the youthful servant gave her a strange, frightened look.

She called out to him, "Where is Barnabas?"

"In the cellar," Willie said. "He'll be up in a few minutes."

She went on to the living room and waited there by the soft light of the flickering candles. Then she heard the voices of Barnabas and Quentin mingling as they came up the stairs.

Barnabas was the first to enter the room. "You got here ahead of us," he said.

"Yes. Is there any news?"

Quentin had now joined them, a grim look on his brown-skinned face. "Not the kind you want to hear," he warned her. "Some newcomers arrived to take residence at the house of Olivia Warner today."

"Who?" she asked.

"I don't know," Barnabas said. "I've just been down in the cellar finding some silver bullets for Quentin's gun. They're the only kind that have any effect against a vampire."

Quentin produced the gun and weighed it in his hand. "I now have a half-dozen silver bullets in this. So let the vampires beware."

"At least it gives you a little more protection," she said.

"Gives us all that much more of an edge," Quentin agreed, putting the gun away in his back pocket again.

Barnabas said, "I'd like you to feel out the temperatures at Collinwood. Neither Quentin nor I dare put in an appearance with anger running so high on Roger's part. But he's bound to welcome you if you're alone and perhaps tell you some things of importance."

"I'll go if you honestly think it will help," she said. "But I'll be nervous there on my own."

Quentin smiled at her. "No need to be. You have a staunch friend and admirer in Roger. Didn't he practically ask you to marry him?"

Barnabas said, "He did, indeed. So you need have no fear at Collinwood. I'm going straight in to the village to try and discover who the new arrivals were today."

"I'll worry about you," she protested.

"No need," Barnabas said. "I'll not be alone. Quentin is going to escort you to the entrance of Collinwood and then he'll go on into the village to join me."

"You must both be cautious," she told them.

"We shall," Barnabas agreed. "And so must you. When the time comes for you to return to this house, be sure that Roger or someone at Collinwood comes with you. You are not to venture out in the darkness alone."

"Very well," she said.

Quentin laughed. "That will be no problem. Roger will fall over himself for the opportunity of seeing her home."

"I hope so," Barnabas said.

They talked for a few minutes and then she kissed Barnabas farewell and she and Quentin went out to get in his tiny car for the short drive to the main house. She settled dejectedly in the front seat beside the shaven headed young man.

"I feel we're all in dreadful danger," she said looking out at the darkness as they drove.

"You mustn't be scared," Quentin said.

"I can't help it!" She gave a tiny shudder.

Quentin spoke from behind the wheel. "That's because you're in love with Barnabas. Our love for another can make us cowardly through our concern."

"You're a great cynic," she accused him.

"I prefer to think of myself as a realist."

"Whatever you call yourself, you have few illusions."

"Is that bad?" he asked her. "I think I'd be much better for you than Barnabas. He's a romantic! Can you imagine? He's wandered this world in torment for nearly two centuries and yet he's still retained his belief in the good of things."

"I admire him for that."

"It will bring about his ruin one day," Quentin predicted. "You need someone who will look at life with hard, clear eyes. Someone like me. And I have an idea Julia would find a cure for you if she was certain it was me you loved rather than Barnabas."

She stared at his profile in the semi-darkness of the car. "Quentin! You must be joking! You know I like you, but it's Barnabas I love."

"It's this cursed disguise," Quentin mourned in a semi-comic fashion. "If I hadn't shaved my head and dyed my skin brown you'd never have given Barnabas a second glance."

"You know that's not true!" she protested in a friendly tone.

"So Barnabas wins once again," Quentin sighed as he halted the car near Collinwood.

"This is far enough," she said, touching his arm affectionately. "Take care of yourself and Barnabas in the village tonight."

"Don't be concerned," he said. "And be careful not to start

home alone."

"I will," she promised as she got out of the car.

She waited until he drove on before she walked the short distance to the entrance of Collinwood. It was important that Roger not notice the car and suspect the presence of Quentin in the old house. As she stood on the steps waiting for the door to be answered she felt strangely afraid. Glancing nervously into the darkness around her, she wondered why she should feel this extra alarm.

The door opened and Elizabeth let her in. She was dressed in a lovely gold hostess gown trimmed with black fur at the sleeves and bottom. "How lucky that you decided to call tonight," Barnabas's lovely cousin exclaimed. "We're having company."

"Then I won't stay. I don't want to intrude," Adele said.

"Nonsense! We'd like you to stay. These people are bound to enjoy you. Come and see Roger for a moment before they arrive."

Elizabeth led her into the elegant living room where Roger Collins was standing by the sideboard in a dinner jacket. He turned to greet her with a smile of surprise on his usually stern face.

"It's good to see you," he said, coming to her. "You've been avoiding us."

"Not really," she said. "I've not been feeling too well."

Roger frowned. "How are your treatments coming along with Julia?"

"She's helping me," Adele said.

"Good," Roger said. "You know the trouble we've been having here. I've been almost convinced that Barnabas is giving refuge to that renegade Quentin. I met Willie in the yardway today and questioned him. He behaved in a very guilty fashion. Do you think Quentin might be hiding in the old house?"

"I don't think he's hiding there," Adele answered truthfully, for as far as she was concerned he was staying there quite openly.

Roger sighed. "There are things I can't explain to you. But Barnabas has me worried. These attacks on the young women in the village are similar to some that happened a year or two ago. Far too similar! And last night one of the newcomers to the village complained of a man appearing on her veranda and then suddenly assuming the shape of a wolf. It terrified her. You may have heard of her, Olivia Warner."

"Yes," she said. "I have." So the fat woman was deliberately spreading malicious lies to harm Quentin and the rest of them.

The doorbell rang and Elizabeth turned to her brother and said, "You answer it, Roger. They are your friends and they'll expect you to greet them."

"Very well," Roger said, straightening his black tie and looking smug. "Charming people. I've just met them. Be back in a minute."

As he went out Elizabeth said to her, "Where is Barnabas tonight?"

"He had something to do in the village. And he wasn't too sure whether Roger would welcome him or not."

Elizabeth shook her head. "That Roger! You know how he is! Utterly unreasonable at times."

Just then Roger returned smiling with his guests beside him. Adele stared at them in utter disbelief. One of them was a dark, sleek young man and the other was the Countess Dario, whom she'd known at the clinic in Switzerland as Lisa!

CHAPTER 11

There was no doubt that the attractive woman she'd known as both Lisa and the Countess Dario recognized her. Adele was sure of that by the expression on her face. She looked interested but wary as she came down the length of the room with Roger Collins.

"May I present Miss Adele Marriot to you, Countess," Roger said. And with a smile her way, "Adele, the Countess Dario."

The Countess, who was wearing a rich black pants suit with a high neck, extended a limp hand to Adele. "How nice to meet you," she said. "But surely you are not a native of Collinsport! Not with that British accent!"

"My home is in London," Adele said, staring into the gleaming, green eyes of the dark-haired woman as she accepted her hand. "I believe we have met before."

The Countess Dario offered her a look of cool disdain. "I think not. I'm sure I would have remembered you. I've spent very little time in London." She held a long, black cigarette holder in her left hand and gestured with it slightly as she talked.

Adele said, "It wasn't in London we met. It was in Switzerland."

"But that's quite impossible!" the frail Countess Dario said with a tinkle of laughter as she took a puff on her cigarette. "When I'm in Switzerland I live in my chalet and I see no one! I really mean no one except when an intimate friend pays me a visit."

"This was in a clinic near Zurich," Adele insisted.

"Sorry," the woman in black said. "You are mistaken. May I present my friend, Charles Breton, Adele Marriot."

The sleek young man bowed over Adele's hand and kissed it. And she felt that his lips were cold. Ice cold! "Charmed," he said, his eyes meeting hers as he lifted his head. They had a weird light in them.

Although the young man's rather narrow face was classic in its lines, there was a weakness evident in him. Everything about him suggested sinister evil to her. She was almost certain he was one of the living dead, while the Countess Dario had been cured of her vampire state through the operation which had left Adele in the shadow of the curse.

Countess Dario at once turned to Roger and began engaging him in a lively conversation about the history of the Collins family. She showed a great interest in it which Adele was inclined to think was pretended. The dark young man stood politely between her and Elizabeth.

Elizabeth asked him, "When did you and the Countess meet my brother?"

"I did not meet him until now," Charles Breton said. "But the Countess called on him at his office this afternoon when she arrived in the village. A business acquaintance had mentioned him and suggested she look him up."

"How fortunate," Elizabeth said. "We enjoy meeting newcomers. Do you expect to be here long?"

"For quite some time if all goes well," the dark young man said with a smile for Adele. "You see, we plan to open and operate a health clinic at Miss Warner's place. A spot like those you find in European health spas. If it catches on we will establish a number of them in the many resort towns in this country."

"It sounds like an excellent idea," Elizabeth said. And she asked Adele, "Don't you agree?"

Adele gave the young man a sharp look. "What sort of clinic is it to be?"

His narrow face lost its smile for a moment. "It will be directed to a wealthy, private clientele," he said carefully. "We hope to announce the appointment of a famous European specialist as our director. A man who has great success in transplants as well as in treating neurotic disorders."

"Would I know him?" Adele asked, wanting to hear Spivak's name.

But Charles Breton was being wary. He offered her another of his charming smiles and said, "I fear, Miss Marriot, the name must remain a secret for a while. We are counting on a great deal of publicity from the announcement."

Elizabeth said, "So much depends on publicity these days."

"True," the young man said.

"What is the role of the Countess Dario in the project?" Adele wanted to know.

"She is a fabulously wealthy woman who has a firm belief in the treatment we are to offer," the young man said. "She herself has gained from the skill of our head doctor to be. And she is providing much of the financial backing for the clinic."

Adele glanced over where the Countess and Roger were standing talking. She said, "The Countess shows no sign of illness now."

"She has recovered," Charles Breton said in his cautious fashion. "But her illness was serious and even classed by some as incurable."

"I'd call her a beauty," Elizabeth said. "And she seems to be getting along extremely well with Roger."

"I'd say so," Adele agreed.

"How do you come to be here, Miss Marriot?" Charles Breton said. "You must have some interest which brought you to this remote place."

The question put to her so suavely caught her unprepared. "I came to visit Collinwood," she said at last.

Elizabeth smiled. "We tried to convince her she should be our house guest here, but she refused. She is staying with our Cousin Barnabas, he also is from London."

"Barnabas!" The young man repeated the name uneasily. "I think I have heard mention of Barnabas Collins. Why?"

Countess Dario had forsaken Roger and come to hear the question. She gave a meaningful look. "But of course you have heard this Barnabas mentioned by Olivia. He is the one they think attacks the young village girls."

Roger had followed the Countess in time to hear her statement. Looking distressed, he said, "I hope you don't have the idea we encourage Barnabas to come here. My cousin has a deed to the old house through a legacy. We cannot stop him from using the place or from coming and going as he likes."

Countess Dario turned to him. "But what an unfair will."

"I agree," Roger said. "I have tried to have it broken without any success at all. So this debauched cousin continues to flaunt his privileges here in my face."

Elizabeth's face had drained of color and she was looking

more upset each moment. She spoke up, "Roger isn't being completely fair. I think he is doing Barnabas an injustice. Most of this talk is gossip and nothing more! We have yet to have anyone come forward and say they witnessed Barnabas in the vampire act."

Roger scowled. "It is common knowledge!"

"Common gossip," Elizabeth said. "No one can prove a thing. And until they are able to do so, I suggest that you not accuse our cousin of these dreadful crimes."

Adele felt like applauding her. But she confined her support to saying, "I know Barnabas well and I don't think him capable of anything of that sort."

Roger looked purple-faced and forlorn. "He has charmed both of you. It is one of his tricks. Women rave about him—until they have reason to fear him, which usually happens soon enough."

"I am sorry," the Countess said. "I believed this was a proven fact. Otherwise I would not have mentioned it. It is a strange village. There is said to be a werewolf at large as well!"

Roger gave Elizabeth a grim glance. "Deny that if you can!"

Elizabeth held her head high. "I have never tried to deny what I know to be true."

The sleek Charles Breton spoke up, "In Yugoslavia we are familiar with both vampires and werewolves. They are part of local legend. But I did not expect to come upon this in America."

Adele said, "I think America may surprise you in many ways."

The pretty Countess Dario turned to her and said, "Is that your feeling about this country?"

"I'm grateful for the hospitality shown me here," Adele said quietly. "And I'm fascinated by its traditions."

Roger was obviously making an effort to regain some of his good humor. With a difficult smile he said, "I have been trying to persuade Adele she should decide to live here."

Countess Dario's green eyes mocked Adele as she said, "I hardly see her in the role of a small village matron. She appears to me more the wandering type and a night person. Have I come anywhere close to reading you rightly, Miss Marriot?"

Adele was convinced this was the girl she'd met in the clinic and the one whom her glandular tissue had saved from being a vampire. She said, "It's not entirely a fair reading. Perhaps it is more an impression. I had a rather odd one about you when we were first introduced. I had the feeling your name was Lisa. Don't ask me why."

"I won't," the Countess said curtly and turned her back to

her as she began further animated conversation with Elizabeth. The sleek Charles Breton joined in, so that Roger and Adele were left free to move away a little distance for a private chat.

"Her mention of Barnabas was terribly embarrassing," Roger lamented.

"I'm on Elizabeth's side in that," she said frankly. "You are too quick to blacken your cousin's name."

Roger sighed. "Of course he has shown you his best side. But if he is what they claim, he has a vile streak in him."

"I would try not to discuss it with strangers," she said.

The stern man showed surprise. "But the Countess Dario is not a stranger! She is my guest!"

"You've only known her since this afternoon. And the young man admits he never met you until tonight."

"That doesn't matter. They come here with excellent references. Mrs. Warner, their hostess, has established fine credit with the local bank. The Countess is a woman with a title."

Adele smiled thinly. "I'm afraid that in Europe titles are much more common and not so respected."

"But surely the Countess Dario is respectable!"

"I hope so," Adele said. "But in this case I also need evidence. And the state of Mrs. Warner's bank credit is not enough for me. Money does not always mean respectability."

Roger seemed shocked. "I hadn't thought of it in that way."

"And are you ready to allow these people to establish a clinic in the village without knowing the name of its director or its exact nature? A clinic for the mad would not be ideal for the middle of the village!"

He gasped. "I should say not." He glanced over where the others were talking and said, "You don't think they have anything like that up their sleeves?"

"You shouldn't give them your approval without finding out."

"That's true."

Adele said, "I'm sorry if I've spoiled the evening for you. But I would say these people are moving too fast to try and gain your good will."

"I'll not endorse their clinic until I know more," Roger said.

"Please be firm about that," she said. "They'll try to sway you."

"I can be firm when the occasion demands it," he promised her.

And for the balance of the evening he showed less enthusiasm for the Countess and her suave male friend. Adele hoped this was a good sign and prayed this might be the first step in exposing the group around Olivia Warner for what they were—part of a ruthless international gang of confidence people.

At last the time came for the party to break up. The Countess and the young man had come in their own limousine. The Countess smiled as she drew her white mink coat around her and said, "Charles is a fabulous driver! Even on these dangerous icy roads."

The swarthy young man looked pleased. "I have had plenty of experience with such roads in Europe," he said.

"What about you, Miss Marriot?" the Countess asked innocently. "Did you drive here?"

"No," she said, suddenly uneasy. "I have only a short walk to another house on the estate."

"But you mustn't walk alone on this cold night!" the Countess protested.

She knew that both Barnabas and Quentin had warned her to get Roger or someone equally responsible to accompany her back home. And now this weird Countess was saying the same thing but not for any good reason. She was certain of that!

Roger said, "I'll walk you home. I'll get my coat."

"But, no!" the Countess protested, raising her hand. "That is most silly! Charles and I shall drop her off and then we'll proceed to the village."

Fear tightened Adele's throat. "No," she said. "I don't want to bother you."

"No bother at all," Charles Breton said with a smile. "I shall deem it a privilege."

Elizabeth smiled agreement. "You may as well accept their kind offer, Adele."

The clamor of their pleasant voices rose in her ears. Everyone was being so kind and protesting that helping her would be a delight. It was like a terrifying nightmare in which you found yourself walking into a trap. She knew that once she entered that car she would be their captive. That they would make her their prisoner. Kidnap her without mercy and have an alibi ready when her disappearance was noticed. These were the smoothest of crooks.

She heard herself saying, "I can walk alone."

"Of course not!" Roger said heartily, shoving her close to the Countess. "You mustn't refuse this kindness on the part of these good people."

Adele wanted to scream they weren't good people. But no one would have listened to her if she had. The babble of talk went on around her as they moved toward the shadowed hallway and the door. Frantically she glanced up at the fine portrait of Barnabas hanging there, his noble features so placid. If only he were here to help her.

Charles Breton had already gone out to get the limousine and bring it around to the front. And the Countess had her arm linked grimly in Adele's so she could not escape. And now they went out onto the steps and there were general good nights. The Countess led Adele toward the car, where Charles stood with the rear door open and a strange, sinister expression on his weak, good-looking face.

There was a moment when she tried to tear away from the Countess. But Charles took her other arm. Between them they literally shoved her into the cavernous back seat of the car. She stumbled into it and sank trembling as a grim-faced Countess came in to join her. Charles closed the door and came quickly around to take his place behind the wheel again.

The Countess told him, "Drive toward the old house. Stop briefly. But don't let her out. Then head to the village as fast as you can. Olivia will be pleased to see who we have for her!"

So now the truth was in the open. Adele listened with a sick heart. She gave the Countess a frightened glance. "You are Lisa, aren't you?"

The Countess replied with a cold smile. "We'll have lots of time to talk about that."

"In the clinic! You spoke about opposites! And I was your opposite! I saw you on the operating table when they wheeled me in!"

"You're talking madly," the Countess said as the big car drew close to the old house. And to the young man at the wheel, she went on, "Halt for a moment so if they're watching they'll be sure we let her out."

Adele said, "You won't get away with this. I have friends now to help me."

"You bore me with your lies," the Countess told her as the car swung in a circle and came to a brief halt before the old red house.

Then as Adele felt she was facing her moment of greatest despair, a shadowy form rose from the darkness of the floor of the front seat. And the shadowy form took shape in her eyes as Barnabas!

"Don't start the car again, Charles," Barnabas said in a taut voice. "I have my gun pointed at you. It is filled with silver bullets and one of them will surely lodge in your vampire heart if you disobey me."

Charles sat motionless and silent behind the wheel.

Countess Dario screamed angrily. "How dare you hide yourself in my car?"

Barnabas turned to her coldly. "The less you say, Countess, the better for you. I don't care in whose body these silver bullets lodge."

"You criminal!" the Countess gasped.

"I find that funny," Barnabas said. "Get out, Adele."

"Thank you, Barnabas," she said. And she did.

A moment later Barnabas joined her and the car drove off. He gave her a grim smile. "For once I had a hunch that worked out."

"How did you guess?"

He gazed after the vanishing taillights of the big limousine as it zoomed off into the darkness in the direction of Collinwood. Then he took her by the arm and said, "Let's go inside where we can talk comfortably."

Quentin was waiting for them in there. "Did you find a use for my gun, Barnabas?" was his first question.

"Exactly as I expected," Barnabas said, and he took out the gun and returned it to Quentin.

Adele looked from one to the other of them with admiration. "How did you guess what would happen? That I'd be in danger?"

Barnabas smiled at her. "The first thing we did was find out that three or four new people came to join Olivia Warner today. And one of them was called the Countess Dario."

"We had a few drinks in the Blue Whale and Roger's elderly male secretary told us that the Countess had called on Roger today and he'd invited her and an escort to Collinwood tonight," Quentin explained.

"So then we knew the Countess and an accomplice would be guests there with you," Barnabas said.

"And you had an idea she'd try to kidnap me?" Adele questioned.

"After last night it seemed most likely," Barnabas agreed. "So when we drove back, I borrowed Quentin's gun and walked to the limousine and hid in the front seat. That Charles fellow knew from the start but he didn't dare warn the Countess, as I had the gun pointed to fire all the time."

"You saved my life!"

"At least we spoiled their little plot," Barnabas said modestly.

"I'd like to have heard the Countess and seen her face," Quentin laughed.

"She was livid!" Adele said.

"They're not finished yet," Barnabas warned her. "In fact, I see this as only the beginning. The danger for us will grow. And your Countess friend is going to want to revenge herself for the humiliations of tonight."

Adele knew that everything he was saying was right. She told him, "I learned one thing from that dark fellow. They are planning to establish a clinic here."

"I knew it!" Barnabas exclaimed.

"And that Countess is the Lisa I've talked about so much," she said.

"Though she keeps on denying it," Barnabas said with a grim smile. "Well, we'll find out about her later."

"I'm positive she was my opposite in the operation," Adele worried. "Though last night Olivia Warner said her brother, Anton, was the one who received my gland tissue. I still can't believe it. She was lying to throw me off."

Quentin's face was directly bathed in the glow of the candelabrum on the mantel. He gave her a knowing look. "Of course there is one sure way of finding out."

"How?"

Barnabas said, "I think Quentin is referring to Julia Hoffman's theory."

"What is that? I don't remember. It seems she had so many," Adele said.

Quentin said, "It is Julia's belief if you kill the recipient of the gland tissue, the person from whom it was taken will gradually return to normal. All we need do is put a silver bullet or a stake of hawthorn through Anton's heart and we'd soon know whether he was the one or not."

She shook her head. "You'll never get near enough Anton to try that."

"I mightn't," Quentin said with a strange gleam in his eyes. "But suppose it was a huge wolf-like dog that came up to him?"

"Or a large bat?" Barnabas said. "They tell in the village that I can change myself into a bat at will."

"But that's nonsense!" she protested.

Quentin smiled thinly. "Don't be too sure!"

Then Barnabas deliberately changed the subject and they talked of the journey they must make to Julia Hoffman's clinic the following night. But she had the feeling he was only trying to get her thinking along different lines. That he had some definite plan in mind and Quentin was probably a collaborator in it.

The next evening they did drive through a light snowstorm to the clinic several hours distant. When they got there Julia Hoffman was not in the hospital. She'd been called to Boston to assist in an unusual operation there. So Professor Stokes gave Adele her regular examination and had the serum ready for them.

As he gave her the small carton with the precious vials in it, he said. "I would like to see you free from using that stuff."

"There's no other way," she said.

"There is," he told her. "And I don't mean scavenging for throats to drain them of blood. I'm thinking of a cure."

"I can't see any hope."

"Don't be too sure, Miss Marriot," the pompous Professor Stokes said. "From my examination of you today, I believe the vampire taint has lost strength."

The news excited her. It was the first good word she'd had. "What does that mean, Professor?"

His face was solemn. "I have an idea whoever was your opposite in the operation is about to realize they are losing its benefits. And as they lose ground and return to being a vampire, so your state will return to normalcy. It can happen as naturally as that without any surgery or strong medication."

"That's wonderful news!" she gasped.

"The signs are in your tests."

"Is there any way the improvement could be stopped? Could anyone spoil it for me?" she worried.

"No," Professor Stokes said. "Not unless you went through another similar operation with your opposite. Then the benefits would go on longer for them."

"I certainly wouldn't allow that!"

"You were tricked into the last operation," the Professor said. "But you won't be so easily fooled this time."

"You can depend on it," she said bleakly.

The Professor accompanied her to the door of his private office. "If the tests show further improvement on your next visit, it might only be a matter of weeks before you are completely normal."

As soon as she joined Barnabas she told him the news. He was jubilant about it but also worried about her protection. For he was alert to dangers that hadn't occurred to her. And as they drove back to Collinsport in the car he went on to explain them.

He said, "I can see now why they are making these strong efforts to kidnap you. One of them, either Anton or the Countess, is beginning to return to a vampire state as you get better. They need you for a second operation, and that means Doctor Stefan Spivak must be on his way here since he is the only person capable of performing that particular surgery."

She found herself trembling at the picture he was painting. "That young man said tonight a famous European doctor was to head their clinic."

"It has to be Spivak!" Barnabas exclaimed from the wheel.

"But he hasn't shown himself here yet," she pointed out.

"He will," Barnabas predicted. "I'm positive the Swiss authorities closed his clinic and deported him from the country. That's what has driven him and his motley crew here."

She sank back against the car seat wearily. "Anyway, I'm not sure that I want to be cured."

"Don't want to be cured!" he echoed in surprise.

"No."

"You're just saying that."

"I mean it. I'd rather share this fate with you. I can't leave you alone!"

Barnabas sighed deeply but he kept his eyes on the road ahead where the headlights were cutting through the lazily falling snow. "We've been all over that before. You know how I feel."

"I can still do as I please."

"If you disobey me, you'll only win my anger," he warned her.

"Barnabas, I've come to love you," she said unhappily. "I don't want to be on one side of the grave with you on the other. I understand how Julia feels now."

"If you make a natural return to normalcy there is nothing you can do about it," he said. "Maybe one day I'll be equally fortunate."

"What about in the meantime?"

"We must be patient," he said.

She shook her head. "You know that talk doesn't make sense. You hope if I recover I'll forget about you and go back to Douglas Edwards in London. You've even said that I should."

"I think it would be an ideal solution," Barnabas said.

"I won't," she warned him. "If you desert me I'll turn to Quentin. He likes me and he'd take me with him."

Barnabas gave her a warning glance. "That would turn your life into a disaster."

"Next to you I like Quentin better than anyone I've met."

"Quentin is Quentin." There was a weariness in the tone of the man at the wheel. "And anyway, you're taking too much for granted. I know he wouldn't do a thing like that to you. Quentin may be fond of you, but he'd never encourage you to go off with him."

"Keep on and we'll be finding out," she warned him.

They were nearing Collinsport and he said, "I don't feel like going home yet. It's not as late as usual. The Blue Whale is open. Let's go there for a good night drink."

"All right," she said.

They parked their car on a side street and then walked down the steep hill of the main street toward the neon lights of the Blue Whale. The snow continued to fall but it was a light storm. They were across the street from the tavern and about to go over to it when its door opened and two men came out. They stood in the doorway a moment before turning up their collars against the snow and starting up the street. One of them was Charles Breton and the other was Dr. Stefan Spivak!

CHAPTER 12

"So he has finally arrived in Collinsport," Barnabas said grimly.

"We almost came face to face with him," she said, awe in her voice.

"At least now we know."

"Yes."

The two men had vanished up the street before she and Barnabas crossed over to the Blue Whale Tavern. The busy gathering place was crowded as usual. A jukebox was playing loudly and the air was filled with blue smoke. Barnabas led the way past the crowded bar ignoring the occasional curious glances they received and found a tiny stall for them at the rear of the place. The waitress came and they ordered. The drinks meant nothing to them and would likely not be touched, but this gave them a place to sit and observe what was going on.

Adele asked, "What do you think will happen next?"

"It's hard to say," Barnabas told her. "One thing we can be sure, Spivak is not a welcome addition to the village."

"He's apparently moved his operations here. And that can only mean trouble for everyone."

Barnabas nodded. "He's taking advantage of the fact no one here knows the macabre nature of his work."

"It will be a rude discovery when they find out," she said.

His eyes met hers in a knowing look. "And we are the two most able to expose him and his ruthless associates."

"Which should make us prime targets for attack by them."

"I agree," Barnabas said. "And you are in double danger because some one of that group needs a second operation from you to save them from lapsing into the vampire state again."

"Olivia Warner claimed it was her brother. My guess is that it's Lisa. In any case, Stefan Spivak is committed to attempting the operation."

"There can be no question of that," Barnabas agreed. "This Countess Dario or Lisa, whichever you call her, has sought out cousin Roger to get his blessing oh their wicked project."

"I warned him about that," she said. "And I think I made at least a small impression on him."

"Then that's a start," Barnabas said grimly.

Their drinks came and the crowd began to thin out a little in the hot, busy traven. She was seated so that she had a view of the front end of the place and the entrance. All at once she saw something which sent a shadow of fear across her pretty face.

"Look up at the end of the bar," she told Barnabas in a low voice.

He turned and glanced over the top of the stall and then gave her a worried glance. "Do you suppose they saw us?"

"They pretended not to. But they must have. Otherwise why would they have sent him here?"

She referred to the massive Anton Warner, who had come into the tavern and was now leaning against the bar. But he was watching them from his position of vantage. His small evil eyes were fixed on their stall.

"He's watching us every minute," she said, leaning across the table and speaking in a low voice.

"That's why he's here," Barnabas said.

"He daren't cause any trouble inside," she said.

"No danger that he will. He's only here to keep an eye on us. The trouble will come when we leave and go to our car. We're parked on that lonely side street."

Her eyes were bright with fear. "What can we do?"

His handsome face was placid. "I have Quentin's gun with the silver bullets. If Anton attacks us and is a vampire, a silver bullet in his heart will fix him. If he should be normal the bullet will work just as well."

"Then you'll be involved in a shooting, perhaps a murder," she worried. "You can't risk it!"

"I'll have no choice if he comes after us."

She said, "We could get the tavern owner to call the police."

"And what would we say? That we think we might be attacked? I doubt if they'd listen to us."

"There must be something," she worried.

"We'll play it by ear," he said. "It's the only way."

Adele glanced up at the bar again and in a taut whisper told Barnabas, "He's gone!"

Barnabas looked. "He didn't stay long."

"He just wanted to make sure we were here," he said. "He couldn't order since he can't speak properly. He makes a kind of growling noise."

"A regular monster," Barnabas said with a grim smile. "Almost as charming as his overweight sister!"

"Don't talk about them!" she pleaded.

"We'll wait a little longer," Barnabas said. "Then we'll start out and hope that we make the car safely."

"They know where we are and the way we have to come out," she sighed. "It will be easy for them."

"Not all that easy," he said. "I won't give in without a fight. If it comes to that you'd better try to get in the car and escape."

"And leave you alone at their mercy?"

"I'll survive."

"I'm not all that sure," she complained. "We'll face this together or not at all."

"I appreciate your loyalty," Barnabas said, "but I deplore your judgment." They sat in tense silence for an additional few minutes. Then he told her, "Time to go."

The tavern was almost empty as they made their way out. They left the fetid warm air and the stench of smoke for the brisk salt air outside. The snow still continued to fall in a lazy pattern. Storms of this type often could last a day and night without depositing much snow on the ground. Like most of the tavern's customers, they hesitated in the doorway for a few seconds.

"Let's make a dash for it," Barnabas said, taking her arm.

"Don't allow us to be parted," she cried as they raced across the street toward the dark side street where the car was parked.

She saw the car ahead and felt that they had been lucky after all. Anton's coming into the tavern might have been a mere coincidence. As Barnabas gave his attention to unlocking the car door she was about to say this, but before she could the huge bulk of the monstrous Anton came rising out from behind the car to attack them. "Barnabas!" she screamed.

The man in the caped-coat whirled around, the gun holding the silver bullets in his hand. He fired directly at the chest of the giant. Anton stood motionless for a second, then clasped his hands to his chest and with a low growling sound toppled to the snow-ridden ground. And as Adele watched in silent horror, the massive frame seemed to wither and shrink until it looked to be no more than normal in size.

Barnabas stood grimly over the fallen Anton with the gun still in his hand. He used his foot to roughly turn the body over so that the withered, ancient face of the once massive Anton was revealed. "He was one of us!" Barnabas said grimly. "One of the living dead. The silver bullet was what we needed."

"What now?"

"Leave him here," Barnabas said. "They'll come looking for him."

"And we'd better be gone before they do!"

"Exactly," Barnabas said, opening the car door for her to get in.

She was still shattered by the incident when they reached the safety of the old house. As they walked from the car she realized she was trembling. Inside, they found Quentin waiting for them in the living room.

He greeted them with, "You must have had an interesting session with Doctor Hoffman tonight. You're late."

"We had an interesting session, but not with Julia," Barnabas said. And he told him about their encounter with Anton.

Quentin looked amazed. "So you actually destroyed him!"

"Yes," Barnabas said. "I had no choice."

"That will do it," Quentin said. "The fat woman had an insane devotion for her monster of a brother. She'll insist that Spivak seek revenge for his killing or refuse to cooperate with him."

"That's very possible," Barnabas agreed.

"I'm terrified," Adele confessed.

"You have every reason to be," Barnabas agreed. And he explained to Quentin why Spivak and the others were so anxious to kidnap her for a second operation. One of the leaders of their group would revert to the living dead without her tissue.

Quentin's brow furrowed. "It can't have been Anton as his sister said; he was already a vampire."

"I knew she was lying," Adele agreed.

"So your opposite probably is Lisa," Barnabas said. "And she must be desperate to see you on that operating table again. She knows she is slipping back from her recovery."

"What about the police?" Quentin asked.

"I doubt if they'll report the murder," Barnabas said. "If they have to produce Anton's body, the police will suspect something. He withered to a weird, mummified state before we left him. They wouldn't be able to account for that, so they'll probably just bury his body in the cellar of the house."

She said, "At least that will spare us a police investigation."

"But we'll still be the main targets for their vengeance," Barnabas said. "We must expect that."

"It's a battle to destruction," Quentin suggested. "You mean to remove them from Collinsport and ruin their diabolical schemes and they are just as determined to eliminate you both."

Barnabas gave him a weary smile. "I'm afraid you must include yourself in our camp. I'm sure they do. And they'll not be satisfied until they've settled with you as well."

"That is all right with me," Quentin said quietly.

They talked in sober tones for a little longer and then she went up to her bedroom to await her daylight sleep. She was tired of this restricting experience and hoped that soon she would be freed from it and normal again. But only if Barnabas also was cured. Finally, she slept.

When she awakened she was at once faced with a shock. She was no longer in her own bedroom and she was bound at the hands and feet. She tried to wriggle free of her bonds without managing it. Filled with terror, she stared around her in the darkness and could make out nothing. What had happened?

Her answer came sooner than she'd expected. A door opened from a lighted hallway and then a light was switched on in the room she was in. And the fat Olivia Warner waddled over toward her accompanied by Dr. Stefan Spivak. Adele looked up at them from the cot on which she was a prisoner and she was further alarmed by the hatred on the jowled face of the weird woman.

Olivia jeered at her. "How do you like your new quarters?"

"How did I get here? What right have you to tie me up?" she demanded.

Dr. Stefan Spivak moved nearer and smiled down at her. "So nice to see you again, Miss Marriot. We needed you desperately for another experiment and so some of my people staged a raid on the old house while both you and Barnabas were deep in the sleep of the dead. And then we brought you here."

Her eyes widened with fear. "What about Willie and Quentin?"

The wily doctor smiled coldly. "You expected them to guard you?"

"I'm sure they did. What have you done to them?" she demanded.

He said, "We took pains to wait until Quentin went to the village on an errand. Willie was not all that hard to handle. A heavy blow on the head put him out of the running and left you and Barnabas at our mercy!"

"Where is Barnabas?"

Olivia Warner gave a nasty chuckle that set all three of her jowls rippling. "He's in the room next to this. And when the time comes, we'll let you watch while we drive a stake of hawthorn through his heart. The wanderings of your beloved Barnabas are about to come to an end!"

"No! You mustn't!" she pleaded.

"Why not?" the fat woman demanded angrily. "That is what he did to my brother!"

"Your brother attacked us. He gave us no choice!"

Dr. Stefan Spivak looked smug. "I fear we had no choice but to send Anton after you. I know you and Barnabas meant to expose us and drive us from this new haven as we were driven out of Switzerland. I can't allow that to happen again. South America might offer a last resort refuge, but this village is much better suited for my clientele."

"Quentin will know and come after you!" she warned him.

"We shall deal with Quentin when the time comes," the evil doctor said suavely. "Our problem at the moment is you two. But we have plans for you both. It was very easy to capture you. Vampires are so open to destruction during the time of their daylight sleep. Now it will be the operating table for you and the stake for Barnabas."

"Neither of you will ever leave here," Olivia Warner said with relish.

"We'll allow you to think about this for a little," Dr. Spivak said. "I shall be preparing our new operating room for your arrival and arranging for your opposite to be there."

"You mean the Countess Dario! Lisa!" she said bitterly.

"I cannot divulge that information," he said.

"We'll be back to get you soon," Olivia Warner told her. "And before you go to the operating room you'll watch us destroy your friend Barnabas." With a last chuckle she waddled out of the room.

Dr. Spivak shrugged for Adele's benefit. "I would have tried to be a trifle more humane in my handling of this. But you incurred her wrath when you destroyed Anton. And since I'm greatly in need of her support I must go along with her plans."

"You're the most rotten of the lot!" she told him.

He accepted this with a smile. "I shall have to look on that as a compliment, Miss Marriot." And with that he also left the room, turning out the light when he went.

She lay there in the darkness with her head in a whirl. How could things have gone so wrong? Where was Quentin? He surely must be aware of the plight they were in. Why was he waiting so long to help them? Was he able to help them? Perhaps they had played some cruel trick on him as well. He could easily be dead at this moment.

She was resigned to whatever fate they might have in store for her. But she dearly wished she could do something to save Barnabas. It was she who had involved him so deeply in the affairs of the macabre clinic. And now he was to be destroyed for his kindness to her. It was a heart-breaking thought!

Time passed and then the door opened again. When the light was switched on she saw that her latest caller was the Countess Dario. The dark girl looked pale and strained as she walked slowly over to her. There were deep, black circles under her eyes.

She said, "This time I can admit we met in Switzerland."

Adele stared up at her. "You are Lisa!"

"Yes, I'm Lisa," the other girl said wearily. "What a fool you are to think you can win out against Doctor Spivak. He is one of the great surgeons of our century."

"He's not even a doctor!"

"I don't believe that," the dark girl said.

"Ask him," Adele urged her. "He may destroy Barnabas and me but he'll be exposed before he gets a chance to carry on his evil work here."

"I think not."

Adele said, "You are my opposite, aren't you? And you're sliding back into the vampire state. You think a second operation will save you. But it will happen again and by that time I'll be dead and there can be no third operation. So in the end you'll be one of the living dead. There's no escape from the curse!"

"So you say. Anyway, I'm not your opposite," Lisa said nervously.

"I don't believe that."

"Believe it or not, it's so," Lisa maintained. "I've talked to Barnabas Collins. What an interesting man! Too bad he has to be destroyed."

Adele said, "If you're so taken with him, why don't you try to save him some way?"

"For you?" the dark girl asked sarcastically.

"For yourself. I'll be finished by the time I leave the operating room tonight."

Lisa smiled coldly. "It's a temptation. But I can't think about it."

"Do," she implored her.

"No," the dark girl said. And she left.

Now the waiting became almost unendurable. Adele knew that soon the evil doctor and his cohorts would come for her and she would be taken in to see Barnabas, but only to observe him as he met his death.

What would the people at Collinwood think about all this? Would Willie tell them what had happened or would he be too frightened of Roger's wrath? They would be missed from the old house, but Elizabeth and Roger might take it for granted they had simply gone on their way somewhere!

The door opened and the light was snapped on again. This time Dr. Stefan Spivak was accompanied by both Olivia Warner and Charles Breton.

Dr. Spivak said. "Untie her ankles, Charles. And then bring her on to the next room."

The swarthy young man came over and hastily took the binding off her ankles and then massaged them. He asked her, "Do you think you can stand?"

"I don't know," she said, painfully.

"Well, try," he said, and assisted her to her feet.

She stood shakily before the expressionless Dr. Spivak and a leering Olivia Warner. The fat woman said. "Now we can move on for our visit to Barnabas."

Adele said nothing. She knew it would be useless to plead with the two to spare Barnabas. Her only hope was that Lisa might decide to save him. But when they entered the next room, which had the appearance of a sitting room with a large fireplace in which logs blazed, her heart sank. For Lisa was there standing by a divan on which a bound Barnabas lay a prisoner.

The pale, dark-haired girl greeted their arrival with a grim smile. "It has the air of a party," was her comment.

Charles Breton took Adele over close to Barnabas. She gazed down at his handsome, weary face and felt a rush of despair. "I'm sorry, Barnabas," she said sorrowfully.

He managed a smile for her. "Not your fault."

"I can't help blaming myself," she told him.

Dr. Stefan Spivak came forward and there was a mallet and a slim, pointed stake in his hands. "I must intrude on this tender scene," he said in his suave way. He turned to Barnabas. "In a moment you will be released from your vampire state. You should be grateful."

"I might be if the release came from other hands and for different motives," Barnabas said.

Olivia Warner pushed her monstrously obese body close to Adele. She grinned at her maliciously. "I want you to enjoy every moment of this. And now I have something else to tell you."

She turned away. "I don't want to hear anything from you!"

"You must hear this," the fat woman gloated. "I am your opposite!"

Adele was so truly startled that she turned around to stare at the ugly, squat woman. "You!"

"You were so certain it was Lisa," Olivia Warner said. "But all along I was the one! So now you know. When Barnabas is dead you'll give your life for me."

It was a moment of utmost despair for her. She felt that nothing worse could happen. Then the fat woman said, "With your permission, Doctor, I would like to perform an experiment on Barnabas before he dies."

Dr. Spivak eyed her dubiously. "We shouldn't waste time."

"This won't take long," Olivia said. "I would like to watch how a vampire like Barnabas reacts to pain. I will take a flaming stick from the fire and touch it to his eyes before you use the stake to drill his heart."

"No!" Adele screamed out and tried to free herself of the firm grasp of Charles Breton.

Barnabas frowned for her to be calm. "Don't worry about me," he said. "I have suffered so many tortures over the years anything they can do will be minor."

The fat woman had already waddled to the fireplace. Now she was using iron tongs with long handles to gingerly retrieve a blazing stick from the fire. Holding it a distance from her, she came back triumphantly. Dr. Spivak said nothing, but the look on his hawk-face indicated annoyance at the madwoman's capers.

"Now we shall test the bravery of Barnabas Collins," the woman exulted. "He murdered my poor, retarded brother. He had no pity then! Let us see if he will ask for some now!"

As Olivia slowly approached the divan with the flaming stick, Adele screamed out in panic once more. Charles Breton roughly drew her back. Lisa turned away so as not to have to watch the painful moment. Dr. Stefan Spivak seemed hypnotized into motionless silence by the situation.

Then pandemonium broke loose. Through the open doorway bounded a huge, greenish-gray wolf-like creature. It sprang directly at Olivia and knocked the fat woman screaming onto the carpet. The blazing stick escaped from the tongs and began to burn the rug. It took the monstrous animal only a second to rip open Olivia's throat and then turn its attentions to Dr. Stefan Spivak.

He stumbled back in horror as the furious animal next sprang at him and mauled him with slavering, bloody fury. Its giant teeth ripped the suave doctor's face and clothing. Charles Breton fled from the room and Lisa cringed in a distant corner shrieking her fear!

Adele rushed to Barnabas and quickly untied the bindings at his ankles and wrists. By the time she had him freed, the wolf had left a dormant, bloodied Dr. Stefan Spivak on the floor and raced toward Lisa. It was the cue for her to turn and run to the nearest window and plunge through it screaming. The animal hesitated before the window and, paying no attention to either Barnabas or Adele, bounded out of the room. The rug was blazing and the room was filling with smoke.

Barnabas took her by the arm. "We've got to get out of here fast!"

She looked back at the bodies of Olivia and Stefan Spivak on the floor. "What about those two?"

His arm was around her as he urged her out of the room. "The fire will take care of them," he said.

They reached the head of the stairs of what appeared to be the attic of the old house and started down. They were just in time to see the wolf thing catch up with Charles Breton on the stairway below. The slim, dark young man let out wild screams but only for a moment. The thing had torn out his throat in the matter of a second. Then it bounded on down the stairway leaving the bloodied body of the young man sprawled drunkenly on the stairs.

She and Barnabas had to pass the body with its bulging, terrified eyes. She gave it only a glimpse before she turned away. Barnabas helped her down into the lower regions of the old house. The smoke was spreading and they could feel the heat of the flames from the blazing inferno above. The house was clearly doomed.

He led her out a side door and the air was icy cold in contrast to the heat of the burning house. The side street was beginning to fill with people. There was shouting and cars pulled up as newcomers joined the scene to watch the blaze in the middle of the grim winter night.

They kept in the shadows of the house so as not to be seen by those on the street before the old building. And then from the darkness there came the familiar figure of Quentin.

"Follow me," he said. "I have my car on the other street."

And they rushed after him, pushing back some snow-tinged hedges as they made their way across another property to the next street, which was deserted except for Quentin's car. He had the door open for them. They got in and he slid behind the wheel and drove away.

She stared at his stern profile as he sat behind the wheel. The stories of the werewolf she'd heard came back to her. But she couldn't picture this pleasant friend as the wild, murdering animal she'd seen in the room a few short minutes ago.

Barnabas broke the silence. "Thanks, Quentin."

"For what?" Quentin asked. "For leaving the old house and allowing you two to be kidnapped? I was badly in error. Coming to pick you up now isn't all that important."

Barnabas said, "Have it the way you want it. I'd say we've cleaned up Spivak's nest of evil. The fire will eat up their bodies before anyone can get to them. All except Lisa. She jumped to her death."

"She wasn't one of the living dead," Quentin said. "So you can be sure she's dead now after that fall."

"So it's all over," Adele said in a hushed voice.

"Let us hope so," Barnabas said.

They reached the old house and Quentin let them get out, but he kept the car running. The young man leaned out the window. "After tonight I have to be moving on. Good luck, Adele. You'll be all right."

"When will I see you again?" she asked, standing by the steps.

"I'll be around wherever Barnabas is," he said with a smile. "Goodbye for now." He waved, closed the window and drove off.

Barnabas watched after him rather sadly. "We'd best go inside," he said.

A bruised and battered Willie greeted them joyfully. He had a wide bandage on his head. "I knew you'd be back," he exclaimed.

Barnabas took her on to the living room. They stood there facing each other in the candlelight. "You must try to forget tonight," he said. "Blot it from your mind. But you did learn one important thing. Your opposite was Olivia. With the fat woman dead, dawn should hold no terrors for you any longer. You should become normal again."

"I can't believe it," she protested.

"We'll know when dawn comes," Barnabas said. And he touched his lips gently to hers.

He insisted that she go to her own bedroom to await the dawn. If the sleep of death came upon her there as usual, she would be safe. So she was stretched out on her bed waiting as the first rosy glow appeared in the sky. And she was not sleepy! She was free of the curse at last!

She waited a few minutes longer and then rose from the bed filled with joy. She knew Barnabas would be in that deep sleep by now, but she wanted to go to him and tell him the good news even though he wouldn't be able to hear her. At least she would be close to him. And tonight they could make plans.

Rushing downstairs, she heard the sound of a car starting outside. All the windows were shuttered so she had to race to the door. She opened it in time to see the station wagon pulling away. She cried out for Willie to stop the wagon but he paid no attention to her.

Still in a panic, she left the door open and rushed down the dark hall to the cellar entrance. She stumbled down the steps and across the blackness of the dank underground place to the room where Barnabas had his coffin. She leaned weakly against the door frame and saw that the coffin was gone. She could picture him in it in the back of the station wagon!

It was his way of telling her it was over. She would go back to London alone to pick up the strands of her former life. Perhaps she would fall in love and marry, but she would never forget Barnabas, Quentin or Collinwood. Slowly she made her way upstairs. .

Roger Collins in hat and overcoat was standing in the upper hall. He said, "I thought the place might be deserted. I came to tell you of a dreadful fire in town last night. Countess Dario and others were killed. And I passed Barnabas driving away. Or at least his man was at the wheel of the station wagon. I shall miss talking to him."

She nodded. "So will I."

ᴅARK ꜱHADOWS

Published by **Hermes** Press

Visit **www.hermespress.com** to learn more
and see additional *Dark Shadows* titles.

ᚦARK ᚦHADOWS

Published by **Hermes** Press

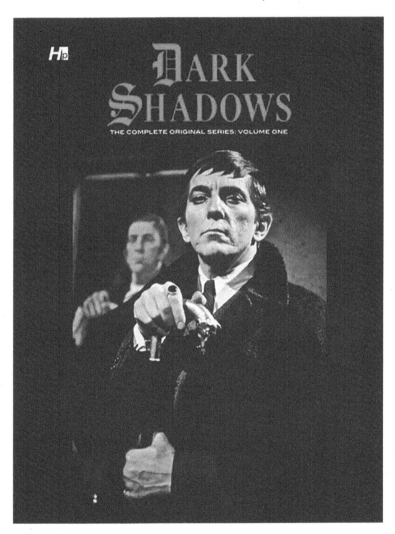

AVAILABLE NOW
Dark Shadows: The Complete Series: Volume 1
SECOND EDITION
From the Gold Key Comics 1968-1970
www.hermespress.com